Confusion was not a familiar state for Daniel. Until now.

This situation with Erin was a no-win wrapped up in a heartache. There was so much on the line. But his daughter was bursting with the pride of finally meeting her mama, and discovering Erin's accomplishments.

At only thirty-four, Erin was a gifted photographer who had been awarded some of the world's highest honors for her work. Daniel was not immune to the impressive allure of Erin Gray and her talent.

True, this Erin might be different from the young woman who'd stood before the justice of the peace with him over sixteen years ago, but when Daniel looked into her eyes, a glimmer of that skittish girl still existed.

He knew her fears, knew her past and knew she would run away to catch up with her future as soon as she got well again.

And that was exactly what he wanted. Or was it?

Books by Mae Nunn

Love Inspired

Hearts in Bloom
*Sealed with a Kiss
*Amazing Love
*Mom in the Middle
*Lone Star Courtship
A Texas Ranger's Family

*Texas Treasures

MAE NUNN

grew up in Houston and graduated from the University of Texas with a degree in communications. When she fell for a transplanted Englishman who lived in Atlanta, she hung up her Texas spurs to become a Georgia Southern belle. Mae recently retired after thirty years of corporate life. When asked how she felt about being a full-time writer, Mae summed her response up with one word, "Yeeeeeha!"

A Texas Ranger's Family
Mae Nunn

Steeple Hill®

Published by Steeple Hill Books™

STEEPLE HILL BOOKS

Steeple
Hill®

Recycling programs
for this product may
not exist in your area.

ISBN-13: 978-0-373-87551-1

A TEXAS RANGER'S FAMILY

A cord of three strands is not quickly broken.
—*Ecclesiastes* 4:12

A Texas Ranger's Family is for my darlin' Michael. Thank you for taking care of me, putting up with me and loving me completely as only you can do. Our twenty-year marriage is proof that happily-ever-after endings occur outside of fairy tales and romance novels. *Psalms* 37:4 tells us to "Delight yourself in the Lord and He will give you the desires of your heart." Honey, with God as the third strand of our braided cord, I have more than I ever dreamed of. You make it all worthwhile. I adore you.

Chapter One

"Erin, are you awake?"

It was only four words, yet the man's accent was vaguely familiar.

"Yes, I am." Erin Gray's heart lurched at the first recognizable voice she'd heard since regaining consciousness in the ICU of Walter Reed hospital.

The thud of footsteps brought him closer.

"I can't open my eyes!" Her cry was not much more than a raspy whisper, excruciating at that.

"It hurts to move, to talk, to breathe. Hurts everywhere!" She'd give in to the panic rising from her gut but even a single wrench would be too painful.

Tight strips of gauze covered her eyes blocking out all light. Her head and shoulders thumped like the blades of a Blackhawk. Bandages weighed her torso down like a lead blanket. She licked sore lips with a dry tongue. Her mouth was desperate for moisture. Her throat raw.

Respirator.

That's right, a nurse had explained something about being on a respirator for almost three weeks.

Three weeks in a medically induced coma!

Accustomed as Erin was to a military cot, the soft contours of a hospital mattress had produced a throbbing low in her back. She was desperate to sit up or roll to one side. But even the smallest voluntary muscle twitch took her breath away, and if she hadn't been told otherwise, Erin would swear she was in a straightjacket.

"Try to take it easy." The kind man gave a gentle pat to her left hand, the only area of her upper body that seemed free of restraints. "It's not as bad as it seems right now and nowhere near as bad as it coulda been. The heat from the truck bomb that hit your convoy in Kirkuk should have blinded you, but you're only dealin' with scorched corneas. The best ophthalmologist in this place says your healin' is right on schedule." His words were reassuring.

"Thank you, Lord," she mouthed. Her one and only talent was photography. Without work behind the camera lens, she'd have no work at all. God was good, her life and vision had been spared.

"What about my arm?" She needed the truth. "I can't move my arm." A disability would end her imbedded service in Iraq, her limb just one more casualty of a foreign war. "Will I—" she couldn't get the words out the first time "—lose it?"

"God was watchin' over you. Any muscle-bound marine would have bled out from that kind of tissue damage, but I hear your commanding officer got you to the medics in time. You're not out of the woods yet, but all signs are positive."

It was critical, but nothing she couldn't overcome.

A plastic straw pressed to her lips and she sipped carefully, then breathed her first sigh of relief since awakening a few hours earlier.

"Thank you…" She waited for him to say a name she felt she would recognize.

"Daniel."

The surprise caught in her ragged airway.

"Yeah, it's me, Erin. Your bureau chief notified us you'd been critically wounded."

Daniel Stabler was the emergency contact she'd listed on the application when she'd first gone to work for World View News. She would have left the form incomplete but the human resources police had insisted. So her ex-husband's name was the one she'd used to fill in the blank.

"I'm so sorry J.D. troubled you, Daniel," she rasped, thinking she'd give her boss a piece of her mind once she was able to yell again. "He should have known you were only to be contacted in case of a life or death situation."

"Erin, it *was* life or death. Nobody expected you to make it." He delivered the news in the steady, calm Texas accent she recalled as pure Daniel. "Your lungs shouldn't be workin' after the fumes you inhaled, and there was enough staph in your body to kill a Dallas Cowboy linebacker. The fact that you're here today is nothin' short of miraculous."

She knew a little something about miracles. She'd tried countless times to trap one in the viewfinder of her Nikon, to capture one on film. She was grateful to be alive, and surely God spared her for a purpose. For work she still needed to do in this world.

"So, if I'm back from the brink of death, whatever

possessed J.D. to notify you now?" She wheezed out the long sentence.

"He called me weeks ago while you were on the flight to the States. We arrived in Washington the day after you did and we've been here ever since."

She swallowed another sip of water, careful not to choke on the revelation. Why would Daniel come? After the way she'd run out on their marriage he had every reason and every right to stay away, no matter the severity of her circumstances. Maybe he needed something?

The lanky young man she'd married so many years ago stood tall in her mind's eye. He was a portrait of good intentions and Southern manners in worn-out boots. He hadn't seemed much more than a boy but he knew his heart's desire just as well as Erin had known her demons. No man ever wanted a family with a happily-ever-after ending more than Daniel. And he'd been willing to give his best shot at what she'd known for a fact was only a fairy tale.

He'd begged her to marry him and keep the child they hadn't planned. Erin was just a college sophomore when she agreed. She tried to buy into the illusion Daniel spun about a happy family, a foreign concept for an orphaned girl raised in foster care. And after seven more months of pregnancy and twenty-three hours of labor, she gave birth to a daughter.

Three sleepless days and nights into motherhood, Erin lost all ability to distinguish the colicky squalls of her baby from the anguished screams of her childhood memories. She coped in the way she learned from growing up with a raging father in the house. Daniel returned from work to find the tiny infant wailing in her bassinet, while Erin lay curled into the dark confines of their small closet.

"Are you crazy? How could you leave her alone?" Daniel shouted above the baby's cries. He could never understand and Erin couldn't have explained at that age.

So she never tried. She recognized her foolish mistake in believing in his ideals.

She could never be part of a family, never even be comfortable with her own infant. The baby deserved a chance to grow up in a safe home.

So Erin ran like the coward she was.

Lying in the hospital bed now, she conjured up the vision that had assuaged her guilt for sixteen years. Daniel's sinewy arms gently cradling his daughter, his head bent close as he whispered comfort to the tiny life flailing beneath a pale pink blanket.

No, there was no chance the man so determined to have the treasure of his child needed anything from the woman who believed staying as far away as possible was the best thing to do for her daughter.

So, why had Daniel come, and more importantly, why had he stayed so long?

"Did you hear me, Erin?" He touched her hand softly to get her attention.

"Sorry, I guess not. The pain meds have my mind wandering between decades."

"That's a good sign. The doc will be happy to hear you've still got a memory."

She had one but only selectively. Long ago she'd resolved to have dreams of her own, dreams so big there would be no room in her grown-up mind for the unbearable recollections of childhood.

"What time is it?" She needed an anchor, a sense of night and day and of what had transpired in the world while she'd been drifting in nothingness, evidently with Daniel close at her side.

"It's after one. J.D. and Dana should be back up from the cafeteria any minute now."

Dana.

The name they'd given the baby who'd inherited Erin's tainted genes.

Erin had left Texas to protect the defenseless life she brought into the world. And all these years later against every precaution to prevent it, that life was about to collide with hers, again.

The creak of a door and lighter steps signaled a nurse's approach. Metal bearings whirred as a nearby curtain eased back so the attendant could check the machines that hovered nearby.

Erin felt helpless as a turtle on its back, completely dependent upon someone else for her most basic needs. The room was silent as she waited for the encouraging voice of the ICU nurse. The footsteps stopped to her left but there was no conversation, no efficient activity, no tugging off of surgical tape or changing of bedclothes. Only the mechanical beeping and humming of machines.

She held her breath as her mind conjured up the worst that could happen in her world of blindness. But nothing in her imagination prepared Erin for the reality beside her in the quiet room.

"Is she awake, Daddy?" The soft voice of a teenage girl drifted across the empty space that was suddenly crowded with expectation.

* * *

Daniel gripped the brim of his Texas Ranger Stetson to mask the trembling of his hands. His heart rattled against his ribs like a diamondback warning off an intruder. Nothing in a dozen years of law enforcement had invoked this visceral response, this quaking in his gut. No drug-ring infiltration or arms-dealer confrontation had imbued this feeling. Where dangerous men had failed to shake Daniel's reserve, this woman lying in Walter Reed's critical ICU had succeeded. Daniel Stabler was afraid. Afraid this moment would mark the unraveling of his world.

He held his worries in check, allowing his Dana her first verbal encounter with the mother who'd been a phantom for sixteen years. J.D.'s call had changed everything. Daniel owed his child the one opportunity she had to see her mother alive.

As the days turned to weeks, his daughter insisted she would not leave without Erin. He'd accepted Dana's proclamation without argument. Even agreed with it since things had been grim at first. But he realized now with shame that he'd never trusted God for Erin's healing. In fact, Daniel had done everything he could to prepare Dana for the inevitability of Erin's death. Now that it was clear she would survive, Dana was insistent upon taking her mama back to Houston with them.

"Daddy?" Dana gripped his forearm, stared up with glistening, hazel eyes. His daughter's face was flushed with excitement over an all-consuming dream about to be fulfilled. Under normal circumstances there was little he wouldn't sacrifice to see this welcome change. His often-sulking sixteen-year-old was inclined toward ghoulish makeup and shrouds of black Goth clothing, looking more like she belonged to Ozzy Osbourne than Walker, Texas Ranger.

"Daddy, what if she can't hear me?" Dana pressed a palm to the anxiety in her throat, giving him a glimpse of fingernails polished black and bitten to the quick.

"I hear you." The response from the bed was raspy.

"What?" Dana's head, dotted with short purple spikes of hair, swiveled toward the sound and then back again. "Did she say something?"

"I said I heard you, which is about the only thing I can still do."

Daniel noted the voice grew stronger with each word. It was time for the introductions he'd never expected or intended to make. He would need the wisdom of Solomon to navigate this situation if it came close to what Dana envisioned.

"Erin, this precious girl is Dana Marie, *our daughter.*" He gave his only child's shoulders a gentle squeeze. "She's been by your bed every hour the hospital staff allowed and quite a few they don't know about. And when she'd let me join the party, I've been here, too."

"That was very kind of both of you." Erin was cordial, reacting more as Daniel had expected than Dana had hoped. "But as you've probably heard, I'm going to be fine so you should get back to your own lives now."

"How can you say that to us?" Dana's words were awash with indignation. She wriggled to be free of Daniel's hold just as she had a thousand times in her young life.

"I've been crazy worried about you!" Dana inched between the mountain of machines and the bed. Hours of questioning the nurses had familiarized her with the workings of all the equipment. She'd overcome all fear of tripping a wire or kinking a hose.

"I've been waiting for you my whole life. And I've been in this room praying for you to wake up for eighteen days! I've counted the tiles on this ugly floor and the metal hooks that hold the curtain to that track thing on the ceiling. I know how many beeps the heart monitor makes between your breaths and how many times your IV drips in thirty minutes. I've watched while they've bathed you and changed your bandages. The scars are wicked now, but they'll be really cool once they heal."

Dana's words gushed out, a torrent of teenage emotion demanding release. She dared to touch her fingertips to the back of Erin's closed fist.

When Dana spoke again her voice was soft, thoughtful.

"I found out that underneath all that gauze your hair is the same color mine used to be."

Daniel's heart ached in his chest like he'd run a wind sprint. There was no sign of his physical attributes in his child. She had long been desperate to find a connection, a simple resemblance to somebody. Her euphoria over the discovery of something as mundane as her mama's hair color had reduced Daniel's sixteen years of single parenting to the value of a toilet plunger. Nice to know it's there but not something to brag about to your friends.

Dana continued, "And I need to see whether or not our eyes are the same, too."

"I'd like to see that myself." Erin relaxed her left fist and slowly rotated her wrist, not exactly welcoming but neither brushing away the touch of the girl who seemed brave and outspoken.

Must have gotten that from her daddy. Erin imagined a female cookie-cutter version of Daniel. Tall and thin, with those naturally expressive brows of his.

"As a matter of fact, I'd like to see anything." Erin tried to make light of her blindness when in truth, the skin on her neck crawled at the thought of being witnessed this way. Broken. Scarred. Vulnerable.

"Waking up to all this is pretty creepy," Erin admitted. "So I'm sorry about what I said before. I appreciate you being here with me."

She tried to make her croaky words sound sincere but the whole situation was like an out-of-body experience. Maybe any moment the going-toward-the-light part would start. No such luck. She was still very much in this life, in this damaged body, in her dark cocoon with her nose twitching from antiseptic cleanser and no ability to scratch.

"Butter bean, let's sit over here and give Erin a minute to rest her voice."

Feet shuffled away from the bed and Erin thanked God once again that her hearing had been spared. It told her that within arm's reach, the most thoughtful man she'd ever known stood sentry. She wouldn't kid herself that his vigil was for her. No, Daniel would provide the best for his child at all cost. But had he ever considered the price might go this high?

Erin certainly never had. Though she prayed often for the husband and child she left behind, it had never crossed her mind that one day they'd cross her path. And now they were a stone's throw away, not that she could toss a rock if her life depended on it. Her bandaged eyes burned with the notion.

A door creaked and more footsteps thumped against the floor.

"Hello, Ms. Gray." Another voice joined the room. "I am Dr. Agawa."

Fabric rustled on the bed as shoes and chairs bumped about. Erin assumed a path was being cleared for his approach.

"I see your Texas visitors are here again today. You are fortunate to have such loyal friends."

"How are you, sir?" Daniel's greeting was personable, followed by the sound of palms slapping together as the men shook hands.

"I am good, Daniel. Excited to see our patient alert, as I'm sure you and Dana are, as well."

The words were like poking a fresh bruise. Strangers had been attending to her most personal needs. Not only had they invaded her privacy, they seemed to have bonded right under her itchy nose. For the first time she felt kinship with the images in her portfolio of suffering individuals helpless to change their circumstances.

"My ophthalmic team has been treating the thermal burn to your corneas. You are healing very well, indeed. Time for a look," Dr. Agawa announced.

"You're going to remove the bandages?" Erin was hopeful and horrified in the same breath. She'd be brought out of this darkness before an audience.

"Yes, and if all is what I expect, we won't reapply them," the doctor reassured her.

An electric motor hummed as the head of the bed began a steady incline. The shifting of her spine and the repositioning of her weight was painfully pleasant. A loud groan accompanied her long sigh.

The movement stopped. "I'm sorry to hurt you," a woman spoke from the foot of the bed. "This is the first time we've raised your head since we brought you out of the coma."

"Actually, it's lovely to change positions. Please continue," Erin encouraged the attendant.

"That is very good to hear, Ms. Gray." The doctor seemed pleased. "Having you upright will make it easier to remove the compresses. I believe you will see fairly well. But if your vision is blurred for a time, do not be overly concerned."

Her heart's naturally slow rhythm shifted like a souped-up Humvee. Her cardiac monitor beeped into high gear. Someone leaned past the bed and turned down the volume.

"There is nothing to fear," the kindly doctor promised.

Fear? There was no way this pounding of her heart was a sign of fear. She'd been calm when she'd photographed the execution of Saddam Hussein. She'd never broken a sweat when her World View crew had come under guerrilla fire in Somalia, and not even a close encounter with Brad and Angelina in a Parisian restaurant had made Erin's pulse quicken.

No, she'd survived the worst fear had to offer at nine years old, when her drunken father had beat her mother to death. Since then there hadn't been a threat Erin couldn't look in the eye while she kept a steady hand on the shutter release.

"May I have a sip of water?"

"I'll do it," Daniel's daughter insisted, shuffling

closer to the bed, rattling more ice into the cup and angling a straw into Erin's mouth.

The liquid was a cool blessing. She curved her lips in a smile of gratitude.

"What was the last thing you recall seeing before your convoy was ambushed?" Dr. Agawa made conversation as he helped to gently raise her head away from the mattress.

"Actually, not much. We were in the middle of an Iraqi sandstorm. Our battalion had pulled to the side of the road outside of Kirkuk to wait for it to pass. The center of those storms is as black as any darkness you've ever encountered. So, we never saw it coming."

Scissors snipped through thick tape and confident hands unwound the long strips that secured soft pads to her eyelids. As she waited for the pressure of the bandages to abate, a warm hand covered her fingers that had gone cold and trembling with anticipation.

Would her eyesight be the price she paid for the talent that had earned her a Pulitzer prize? Had her bizarre drive to validate her life's purpose by capturing a miracle on film come to a fruitless end?

"Ms. Gray, please be patient and keep your eyes shut for a moment longer."

The compresses fell away revealing a sense of light just beyond her closed lids. Then darkness covered her face as the florescent fixtures were extinguished.

"Open your eyes and look toward the ceiling, please," he instructed.

Fluttering her eyelids was wonderful, like a good stretch after a long flight. But as a bright penlight was shone into first one eye and then the other, it was impossible to make out anything. The doctor agreeably mumbled to himself in Japanese before instructing the nurse to turn on the overhead lights one at a time. With the first flash, Erin squinted to adjust to the brightness, then looked in the direction of the person holding her hand.

The tall gentleman beside her was even more handsome than the skinny boy she remembered so well. The heart monitor began to beep loudly again. Daniel reminded her of a grinning but blurry George Strait. Quite something.

The second switch was snapped on and more light filled the room. Erin's eyes cut left and right to find the fuzzy faces of the doctor and nurse who still supported her shoulders. When the final bank of bulbs glowed overhead, she turned her attention to the foot of the bed and focused hard on the girl dressed all in black, glints of silver dangling from her ears. Dana hugged herself with crossed arms that did nothing to disguise a body well-developed at a young age. As Erin found clear spots in her vision, she looked for signs of Daniel's tanned good looks in his daughter. Instead she noted fair skin, a high forehead, a pointed chin and what looked like spikes of purple sprouting from her head.

As Erin's squint locked on a dark gaze, her breathing stopped and her stomach quaked low in her abdomen. She knew those eyes. Up close there would be flecks of gold.

Erin was a little girl again, hiding with her sleeping baby brother in a dark pantry that smelled of rotting onions. Her mother's screams had mercifully ended hours before but Erin had remained paralyzed, didn't dare to make their presence known. Not even to the people who had finally come to help, the adults who were calling her name.

Suddenly the door swung open and amber eyes with glints of gold glared down from her big sister's face. Her look was as accusing as her words.

"I knew you'd be in your hiding place, you little coward! You didn't do anything to help Mama. Daddy finally killed her!"

Erin blinked, expecting her eyes and imagination were deceiving her addled brain. But the proof stood a few feet away and bore no resemblance to Daniel. From what Erin could make out, hair color was the only physical trait she'd passed on to her daughter. The rest of the girl was the mirror image of Erin's older sister.

Alison.

"How soon can I get out of here?" Erin asked J.D. the moment Daniel and Dana left the room to give her some privacy with her boss.

Her Pillsbury Doughboy of a bureau chief was all smiles to see her sitting upright, her eyes unfettered by the bandages. But she was far from enjoying the blurry images around her. The very thought of being so needy and at the mercy of others, even in a hospital, made her insides shiver. Living with troops in Iraq was a whole lot easier than letting someone else call the shots or take control of her life.

"Take it easy, Wonder Woman. You're still looking at another week here, then once they're satisfied with your vitals and blood work, they'll release you to a rehab facility."

Rehab facility. The term conjured up dingy images of an institution filled with those who needed caregivers.

"Not if I can help it," she murmured.

"There's always the option of going to Texas with Daniel and Dana. They're sincere about this, you know. It's all that girl has talked about for days."

Erin closed her eyes against the thought, reflecting instead on all the injuries she had to overcome.

"Let me make sure I got it all straight." She began to recite her list of traumas. "My right arm was half blown off but thankfully reattached and though I'm going to survive my fingers may not. My pelvis is bruised, but not broken so that's reason to be thankful. My corneas are healing but who knows whether or not I'll be able to focus a camera lens again. The concussion from the IED generally produces long-term memory issues so I'm lucky I know my own name." She paused to consider her circumstances, grateful to be alive but beginning to feel the anger of having lost control of her destiny.

"Oh, and the only viable option to my apartment is a nursing home."

"It's called a rehab facility," J.D. countered.

"That's code for smelly, depressing nursing home and we both know it." Though it was shameful it felt amazingly good to gripe a little now that her voice was back.

"Erin, your frustration is understandable. Anyone in your condition would need to vent." He squeezed her hand again. J.D. oozed calm and patience, traits he'd never displayed in the ten years she'd covered assignments for World View. His kindness didn't make her feel any better. In fact, it made the few hair follicles that weren't taped to her skin prickle with worry.

"Sooooo," she dragged out the syllable. "Am I out of a job?" It might not be the question most people in her situation would ask, but work was her life. It was her world.

"Would you please stop imagining the worst?" J.D. sighed loud enough for Erin to hear. The bedside manner he'd worn for her sake was wearing thin. "You have months of sick time and excellent medical insurance. And don't insult either of us with the insinuation that I'd let you get away from World View. You've shown more guts for living embedded with our troops and compassion for victims of war than the UN and the Red Cross rolled together."

When she didn't respond he patted her hand, accepting her silence.

"Kid, I'm sorry to leave already, but the nurse on the other side of the window is waving me out." He pushed his chair away and stood. "I'll be back tomorrow so you can make some decisions. There are nice places in Washington but I thought you might want to get back up to the city so I have a list of New York rehab hospitals to tell you about, too."

"Can it wait a few days?" The idea of being relegated to an institution, no matter how well the reputation, made her empty stomach churn. "I know you want to get home to Mary Ellen and the boys but I'm going to need some time to ingest all this stuff."

"Sure thing, no rush. And while you're laid up, I've got some great reading to keep you occupied."

"Not again, J.D."

He regularly mentioned that there was a box of letters for her in the mail room but she always declined to have it forwarded. She wasn't exactly Annie Leibovitz so what could possibly be in the postal tub besides credit card applications and Publishers Clearing House offers?

He smacked a loud kiss on her cheek and left Erin alone with her thoughts in the quiet room.

Even if only briefly, her situation was hopelessly out of her hands. But life had taught Erin to be a realist. Going home to her third floor walk-up was definitely not doable. She accepted the fact; her only choice was between a stinky nursing home in D.C. and a stinky nursing home in New York. Too bad a sweaty military Quonset hut wasn't on the list. That would make it a no-brainer.

There's always the option of going to Texas with Daniel and Dana. She recalled J.D.'s comment.

Is that truly an option, Lord? she whispered. *After all my years of wandering the world in search of images that will honor You, have You brought me back to make things up to my child? To honor my family?*

Chapter Two

The 767 eased to a stop at Houston's Intercontinental Airport. Daniel slid his laptop into a worn leather case and stepped into the crowded, narrow aisle. He dipped the crown of his Ranger Stetson to avoid the low doorway of the aircraft and was immediately assaulted by a warm burst of muggy air. He merged with the mass of summer travelers, knowing his daughter's flying experience would be a far cry from mundane.

He'd opted to use the other half of his commercial ticket after J.D.'s assurance that Dana would be secure on the pricey chartered Maverick. Neither female had objected, worn out as they all were from debating where Erin should recuperate. She'd been adamant that she wasn't going to a recovery hospital, and determined to pay for professional home care. It had taken her boss to dissuade Erin from such a phenomenal out-of-pocket expense when her family was so willing to help.

Daniel had sought the Word for guidance, afraid he was a loser whichever way Erin decided. Maybe Dana's dream of a family could be fulfilled, even if his had long ago dimmed. She was desperate for this time with a mother reluctant to go into a setting where she would constantly be put on the spot for information. They'd finally agreed between the three of them that Dana would stifle the endless stream of questions and Erin would share when she felt the time was right.

The cards were definitely stacked in Erin's favor but he and Dana agreed privately that a tight-lipped Erin was better than no Erin at all. And frankly, Daniel was looking forward to being the parent willing to talk while Erin accepted the blame for the gaps in Dana's family tree.

Leaving Walter Reed for the trip to Houston this morning had given Daniel time apart from the two women to figure out whether or not to come clean with the rest of the story. So far, no revelation had presented itself and he was okay with that. Daniel had been alone with his secret for so many years that breaking his silence would be like betraying a partner. He'd never even considered it because there would be a high price to pay with his daughter.

And now, with Erin.

For the past week he and Dana had trained for the care of Erin's injuries. Anything less than around-the-clock attention for the immediate present, followed by intense physical therapy could cost the use of her right arm. It was mostly an academic effort on his part since Dana insisted on being the one to do everything for Erin in spite of their near-disastrous first encounter.

Erin was quick to recover from her initial reaction to seeing Dana for the first time, but the damage was done.

"She thinks I'm ugly." Dana cried during their ride

back to the hotel. He comforted his daughter by joking that they hadn't prepared Erin for an eyebrow ring, pointy purple hair and black lipstick. That was enough to make anybody gasp. They laughed it off and let it go, but he knew Dana was hurt.

Still, she wanted to take care of her mama and was of the unshakable opinion that she could fill the role of Erin's caregiver just fine on her own. So, Dana wasn't gonna like it even one little bit that Daniel had arranged for backup. He had imported the only person he could trust to run his house, help out with Erin's needs and keep an eye on his daughter if he had an overnight investigation. But most importantly, this particular backup would prevent the neighbor's tongues from wagging right out of their heads when his mysterious ex-wife moved in.

His not-so-secret weapon was LaVerne Stabler, a one-woman force of nature. She was a home-cookin' and house-cleanin' machine. A whirlwind of efficiency that meant business and wouldn't stand for anything even close to ungodliness. Given the choice, any cowhand or cousin on their West Texas ranch would sooner stomp on a prairie rattler than cross his mama.

Ironically, even though he exposed his daughter to her grandma on a regular basis, Dana still hadn't figured out what everybody else in the Stabler clan knew; life was just easier in general when LaVerne had things her way.

Daniel slung his carry-on bag into the passenger's seat of his oversized SUV, grateful for the diesel guzzler that would allow him to transport the medical equipment that came along with their guest. It was going be an unpredictable time, and Daniel prayed to maintain his peace when he thought about being trapped under the same roof with three women who held the power to rock his world.

"What's *she* doing here?" Dana hissed.

Erin noted the angry slash of scarlet that blazed across Dana's cheeks as she pointed toward the white Cadillac marred by whiskers of red grime on the fenders. Daniel pulled his behemoth SUV into his driveway and came to a stop.

"You invited that old busybody, didn't you?" Dana spoke to her father through clenched teeth.

In the backseat of the SUV, Erin flinched at the accusation. So much of the teen reminded her of Alison. Each time Dana had hovered over the gurney during the flight from Washington to Houston, Erin had battled a gut-deep urge to recoil. She'd feigned sleep most of the way to dissuade any conversation. *She's not Alison* became a silent mantra whenever Erin looked into the girl's eyes.

Daniel released his seat belt and turned to his daughter. "I'm gonna let that slide because you've been through a lot in the last few weeks. And because I had a feelin' you wouldn't think this was a pleasant surprise. But that *old busybody* is my mama and if you ever talk ugly about her in my presence again, I will make you go back to your natural hair and nail color and take out all your earrings. Got that, Morticia?"

"Yes, sir," Dana muttered, faking repentance.

From Erin's position wedged among many pillows, she observed a brief father-daughter discussion on guest protocol and house rules. The teen negotiated like a United Nations delegate. It was evident she was an only child, always respected as if she were an adult. In the few minutes it took them to reach agreeable terms, the narcotics wore off and Erin's right forearm began pulsing pain. With the bulk of the bandages removed, she had regained control of her head and left torso. But her lower back and hips were still locked down and dependent for movement, especially during the killer hours of torture, aka physical therapy.

"Here comes the other third of your care team," Daniel announced.

"Serenity now," Dana grumbled as she spotted the figure headed their way.

A woman of indefinable years and weight lumbered toward the SUV. She had a Humpty Dumpty figure, bigger on the bottom than on the top. Her bleached updo was complemented by scarlet lipstick and a When-I-am-an-old-woman-I-shall-wear-purple caftan. On her feet were matching sparkly flip-flops.

"Dad, Grandma looks like she's going on a cruise."

"Will you let the lady enjoy being away from the ranch for a change? If she wants to treat this like a vacation, so be it."

"Well, howdy! If you aren't a sight for sore eyes." There was no mistaking the natural Texas drawl.

The woman grabbed the door handle and grunted as she pulled herself up onto the driver's running board. She poked her head through the open window to plant a loud smack on Daniel's left cheek.

"I thought my sweet boy would never get home."

She blew an air kiss toward her grandchild and waved a greeting to the backseat. "My word, look at all that stuff." She counted the boxes and bags by pointing a long nail that matched her lip color.

"Grandma Verne, *what* have you done to your hands?"

"They're called press-on nails. I found them in the sale aisle at the drug store and I think they look kinda nice."

While LaVerne turned her right hand palm outward to admire her faux manicure, Dana glanced into the backseat and rolled her eyes upward beneath kohl-smudged lids. Erin pressed her lips together but let her eyes squint agreeably. She had to admit Dana was amusing and the constant self-chatter had made the last week in the hospital pass quickly.

"Let's get everybody inside before the neighbors take an interest," Daniel instructed.

"Too late for that." LaVerne backed away from the SUV while Daniel stepped out. "As soon as I got here on Thursday evening, that pretty young woman across the street came right over to see if you were home."

Erin noted his quick glance up the block and failure to acknowledge the comment. A girlfriend? The throbbing in her arm increased. She was beginning to feel nauseous.

"Excuse me," Erin called. "I hate to break up the reunion but it's time for my meds."

The father-and-daughter team launched into precision drill activity. Car doors slammed, different doors opened, metal creaked and clanked as cases were removed and a wheelchair was snapped into shape. In another moment Daniel was beside her, solid and clean-smelling as he lifted her out of the vehicle. He gently positioned her into the waiting chair and then stepped away from any further contact.

Dana pushed and he walked alongside reintroducing the two women.

"Erin, I'm sure you remember my mama, LaVerne Stabler. And Mama, it's been a lot of years but you know Erin. She won a Pulitzer prize for the pictures she took in Darfur last year."

"Yes, I heard, son. Who woulda guessed that she'd parlay running off into a celebrity career?"

"Mama." Daniel's censuring tone made only the one word necessary.

Erin expected much worse and deserved anything she got. Judging from the way the Stabler jaws clenched, a lot was going unspoken. For now, anyway.

The move-in passed into a welcome haze after Daniel efficiently administered a dose of pain meds into the still-present IV. Antibiotics dripped day and night to finish off the killer staph while wounds healed and bones mended. The constant jostling of the past twenty-four hours had Erin's muscles stinging and her stomach cringing. It was sleep or barf, so she slipped into numb unconsciousness.

Daniel tilted the lamp shade toward the wall so the low light it cast wouldn't disturb Erin's nap. Thick crew socks muffled his steps toward the metal bed frame. He was pleased LaVerne had thought to set up the hospital rental on the spacious sun porch he'd built last fall.

He gave in to the urge to study her face, attributing his curiosity to years of surveillance work that made it second nature. Her skin was clear, but too tanned and weathered for only thirty-four. Her short auburn hair was sleek and seasoned with occasional flecks of silver. Thick lashes fringed her closed eyes and a handful of freckles were her only adornment apart from an application of Dana's tinted lip balm.

From the few photos of Erin he'd found on the Internet, it seemed she still didn't wear much makeup or dress in a manner that would draw attention. Too early in life she'd mastered the ability to blend into the background so she wouldn't be noticed. He figured that served her well as she waited, still as a fence post, for the right moment to take her photographs. From what he'd witnessed of her career over the years, she was bold to the point of being foolhardy, getting shots others couldn't manage or wouldn't attempt.

It was no surprise to Daniel that she'd won so many awards. In a way he was actually proud Erin had made a life for herself, but that made it doubly difficult to deny Dana's growing need to know something, *anything* about her mama.

As Erin's reputation grew, he was almost glad for the terms of the letter she'd left behind in their one-bedroom Austin apartment. She admitted she'd made a terrible mistake in believing she could have a normal life and didn't dare stay another night. Anonymity was all she asked and in exchange she gave up what he wanted more than his own life.

Their child.

At the time, Daniel had no choice but to live with the deal. He'd known Erin was emotionally damaged, but thought he could love her back to health. He'd been wrong. She'd signed and returned the legal papers giving him full custody. Then she'd changed her last name, and for the past sixteen years Erin had been what her daughter could never be. Invisible.

Daniel almost convinced himself that they wouldn't have made it as a family, anyway. Erin had been deeply wounded too early in life. Over the years he'd uncovered what she'd hidden about her past and often felt he knew too much.

If all the secrets, his included, ever spilled out of his tight grip, what a devastating mess it might be. He was playing Russian roulette by allowing her into the life he'd painstakingly built for himself and Dana. But what choice did he have?

"Daddy, what are you doing in here?" Dana whispered as she crept up behind him.

"Checking to see that everything's okay." He adjusted Erin's IV pole a quarter inch to the right.

"She's pretty, isn't she?" Dana asked.

He slipped his arm around her shoulders and looked down into eyes that expected confirmation but needed reassurance.

"Just like you, baby girl."

"What are y'all up to?" LaVerne hissed from the doorway.

Dana waved her grandmother over and allowed herself to be sandwiched as they stood arm in arm voluntarily for the first time in their lives.

Daniel offered a silent plea. *Lord, I sure hope You know what You're doing here.*

The three people Erin saw standing beside her bed were linked in a typical Christmas card pose. Artificial and forced. Family in its "natural" state. She sent up a prayer.

Lord, I put this all behind me years ago. What is Your purpose in dragging me back? I lost consciousness in one battle zone and regained it in another. I hope You know what You're doing here.

"Hey, you're awake." Dana was the first to notice.

"And hungry," Erin replied. She hated dropping such an obvious hint but the flow of conditioned air from the kitchen, positioned next to the solarium, was pulling a mouthwatering aroma right beneath her nose.

"Well, it's probably not as exotic as what you're used to, but it's one of Daniel's favorite meals. Round steak, corn, mashed potatoes and gravy." There was pride in LaVerne's voice. The woman was crazy about her son.

"If by *exotic* you mean an MRE, I'll stand in your chow line any day."

"MRE?"

"Meals Ready to Eat. 'Yummy' freeze-dried military rations," Erin explained to Dana, glad for a safe subject. "Believe it or not, they're pretty decent but I prefer a camel kabob when I can get one."

"Eeeeeuuuuuuuuu!" Dana's face squinted in disgust. "You've eaten camel?"

"Does it taste like chicken?" Daniel asked.

"Not even close," she answered. "It tastes like… *camel*. Really tough and gamy unless you can get a cut from the hump where the meat is less sinewy."

"I don't know about any camel's hump but I've got supper in the kitchen from a cow's rump, so let's eat." LaVerne headed toward the door. "Dana, I need you to set the table pronto, and no back talk."

Dana noted her father's better-do-as-she-says shrug and left the room.

"Would you like a tray in here?" he offered. "It might be too much for you to come to the table tonight, but it's your call."

Hmm… Stay in here alone while they talk about me

*or join them in the dining room while they watch my
every move. Either way, I'm a big loser who needs
somebody to cut my meat.*

As tempting as it sounded to hide out on the lovely
glass-enclosed porch, it was time to get started. Erin jus-
tified her agreement to join them in Houston as part of
her rehab strategy. She'd made up her mind to look at
every task as therapy. The sooner she could function on
her own, the sooner she could get back to active duty.
Behind the camera lens where she could record the lives
of others. It was so much safer than engaging in the
messy stuff herself.

"I'd like to eat with the rest of you, if it's all right."

"Yeah, sure. Just let me get the wheelchair ready."
He started to turn away, too much of a gentleman to
answer any differently.

"Daniel." Erin lowered her voice so the others
wouldn't hear. "Thank you for allowing me into your
home. I know this is as difficult for you as it is for me,
and I promise as soon as I can physically manage on my
own, I'll get out of your life."

"It's Dana's life I'm worried about, not mine and not
yours. I agreed to have you here for her benefit. Stay as
long as you need to and don't leave before you're ready."
He glanced toward the door, took a step closer and
lowered his voice, as well. "But when you're ready,
you're leaving *alone*. Understand?"

"Perfectly."

His narrowed eyes said he meant business. And who
could blame him.

"Dad, if we have leftovers, will you make potato
pancakes for breakfast before church?" Dana pleaded

from the other room where she plunked dishes and flatware on a tabletop.

"Church?"

Dana had talked a lot about their church home. They knew everybody and attending a service would put Erin on display. She was going to have to pass on the very first opportunity to work on mobility.

"Of course," Daniel answered. He leaned close but waited for her nod to signal permission before sliding supportive arms beneath her knees and the small of her back and lifting without effort. As he settled her into the chair and folded a gosh-awful-looking crocheted thing over her lap, his moss-green eyes locked with hers.

"And don't even think about beggin' off. This family worships together. And whether either one of us likes it or not, Erin, for a little while anyway you're part of this family."

Chapter Three

Sunday morning in Texas was nothing like Erin remembered and everything she'd once imagined it could be.

The chatter that echoed in the kitchen was contentious but good-natured. The dialogue between grandparent and grandchild was one disagreement after another with Daniel acting as mediator. But the dichotomy in the conversation never once escalated into the bitter shouts or harsh threats that accompanied dissent in her family experiences.

As with the meal the night before, breakfast around the pedestal-style oak table was a learning experience for Erin while it seemed like a social event for the others. Conversation stayed clear of the elephant in the room. She blessed Daniel, yet again, for obviously having reminded LaVerne and Dana against pressing for details that weren't offered voluntarily.

But Dana deserved to know something, didn't she? Where to start?

"These potato pancakes are a first for me," Erin mumbled over a mouthful of the tasty breakfast.

Dana's fork hovered between her plate and her mouth. "Nobody ever fixed this at your house?"

Erin busied herself managing a fork in her left fist while she considered how much Dana could handle. There was no doubt the girl had been shortchanged without a mother, but on the other hand, Daniel had provided a pretty sweet deal. Their two-story brick home shaded by hundred-year-old pecan trees was in an affluent Houston neighborhood. Since Daniel had brought Dana up in church, it was Erin's fair guess that he also ensured a quality after-school environment. If nothing else the teenager's appearance was evidence she was respected and given free choice in personal areas so critical to one her age.

How could Dana possibly relate to growing up in a home where constant danger and uncertainty prevailed? Best to withhold that insight.

"Nope," Erin answered the question. "I grew up in a cold cereal kind of house."

Daniel sipped coffee, squinting at her above the rim of his oversized cup. The message of his stare would be more revealing on film, but for now it appeared a cross between censorship and curiosity. It was hard to recall how little she'd told him during their brief marriage, but Erin was certain she hadn't shared much prior to the string of foster homes.

"If you think this is good, wait till you have Daddy's pork spareribs. He cooks them all day and uses molasses in the barbecue sauce."

"Don't be giving away all my secrets," Daniel teased, turning his eyes and attention on Dana.

"And there's nothing like Grandma Verne's butt

cake." Dana was clearly impressed with whatever deserved that description.

"Excuse me?" Erin asked for details.

"It's really Boston cream pie," LaVerne admitted with a proud smile. "But it's so loaded with calories that it goes straight to your backside. Hence the nickname given by my daughter-in-law who lives on the ranch."

"Tell me about this ranch." Erin kept their attention diverted from herself.

"Oh, puuuleeeeease…" Dana groaned.

"There will be plenty of time for that conversation. Right now, we've gotta get going or we'll be late for church. Mama, would you please help Dana with Erin's needs while I clean up in here?" Daniel instructed. "I'll have the truck running and the AC on high for you ladies in thirty minutes."

Daniel glanced frequently into the rearview mirror, keeping an eye on his backseat where Dana gave Erin the lowdown on Abundant Harvest. He lifted up a silent prayer of gratitude for his daughter's excitement over their church community. The contemporary sanctuary doubled as a gym where it was a safe haven for hundreds of teens who gathered there on weeknights. Dana served with the youth's music ministry, where she'd become interested in the technical ins and outs of live worship. Of course, it didn't hurt that the high school praise band was one of the hottest in the state. Whatever the reason, it was comforting to know where his kid and her friends were hanging out on nights when she was free to socialize.

"There's a special place reserved for visitors." Dana pointed toward the front of the sanctuary.

"No, thanks." Erin's response was resolute.

She'd been cooperative so far, but Daniel wasn't surprised when Erin declined the front-and-center spot. Clearly, her comfort was in being the observer, not the observed.

As always, the morning's worship and praise was lively. The pastor's teaching on guarding your heart was relevant to the point of being worrisome. And the newcomer welcome after the service was warm and inviting. Daniel was grateful for his years of friendship and counseling with Pastor Ken, so there was little need to explain the sudden appearance of Erin Gray in their lives.

"I've been praying for your recovery since the day Daniel got word of your injuries." Ken Allen had pulled a chair up and sat knee to knee with Erin and held her left hand as he spoke. "But I never imagined you'd be here with us today. God is awesome to bless us with a visit by someone with your talent."

"Thank you." Erin ducked her head, evidently touched by the pastor's words.

"I know it's a bit soon, but would you consider speaking to our graduates before they head off to college? Just let me know when you're up to it and I'll arrange everything."

Erin's eyes sought Daniel's. If she expected him to intervene, she was out of luck.

"Oh, I don't know, Pastor." She slipped her hand from his and ran unadorned fingertips through her hair. "My skills are all self-taught and I don't have any speaking experience at all."

"Even better," Ken encouraged. "These kids don't want a presentation. They just need to hear you talk about your relationship with God and your passion for your work."

"Well, if that's all you have in mind, I guess I could do it in a few weeks when I'm back on my feet."

"Perfect." Ken rubbed his palms together. "We'll see you again next weekend." He stood and clasped hands with Daniel. "I'll be in touch soon, my friend."

"Pastor?" Erin called as Ken was about to greet another visitor.

"Yes, ma'am?" He turned back to her.

"How is it that you know I have a relationship with God?"

"Are you serious?" The light in Ken's eyes was like a gift he wanted to share. "Your work speaks volumes about you. Nobody could capture the Creator's touch like that without knowing Him personally."

Sunday afternoon was peaceful enough. After a light meal each person moved to a private space. Erin's quiet quarters were disturbed only by the half hour chimes of a mantle clock. Even so, she knew it was a temporary calm. She was experiencing the eye of hurricane Stabler. By Monday morning the gale force would appear again as life in the household resumed full speed with their patient at the center of the whirlwind.

Having others care for her physical needs was a humbling experience. Erin was certain she didn't deserve and could never repay Daniel's kindness. He'd said she was there for Dana's sake, but Erin had no idea where to start or how to meet the raw need sometimes revealed in Dana's eyes.

What she *could* do, however, was recuperate in

record time and return to her own lifestyle so Daniel could do the same.

That recuperation started with a private therapist who would visit each morning to focus on strengthening Erin's back and rehabilitating her right arm. It had been nearly severed three inches above the elbow, but the military physicians in Iraq had more than their fair share of experience with the delicate microsurgery. They'd re-attached bone, reconnected nerves and restored blood flow. Erin could twitch her fingers but there was no sensation in them, only numbness. If the feeling never returned, as she'd been warned may happen, how would the loss of sensitivity impact her abilities?

There was only one way to find out and that was to handle her Nikon as soon as she got the green light to exert her arm beyond the blob of putty she was supposed to squeeze constantly.

The cell phone trilled on the bed beside her.

"What's up, boss?" J.D. was the likely caller.

"Wow! Not only a cheerful but a quick answer." He poked fun at her reputation for being on the go with no time to talk.

"And why does that surprise you?"

"Because the number of times I haven't had to leave a voice mail and wait seventy-two hours for you to return my call can be counted on three fingers."

"I have a few more hours on my hands these days since I'm not exactly tied up." She glanced at the IV tube that had her tethered to an aluminum pole. "Strike that. I'm definitely tied up, just not with assignments. But I was thinking about that just a few minutes ago and—"

"Erin," J.D. interrupted, his voice losing its humorous note. "Give it a rest, will ya? There will be plenty of war, pestilence and famine when you've recovered enough to come back. Meanwhile, try to appreciate having this downtime. Read good books, watch chick flicks. Just appreciate the fact that you're alive."

"I know, I know. And I'm grateful that I'm just in a bed and not a pine box. But my work is my reason to get up in the morning, J.D."

"Well, maybe it's time you found a new purpose. Kid, I love the bureau, but Mary Ellen and our boys are what I live for. You're a young woman with plenty of reasons to get out from behind the camera and focus on real life, no pun intended. You need to get to know that beautiful daughter while she still has time for you. Trust me, in a few more years, you'll have to make an appointment to see her."

"Thanks for the advice, Grandpa Walton. Can I ask a favor?"

"Anything."

"Will you ship me some equipment?"

"I'll put that on my To Do list. But the reason I called is to let you know I'm heading for the West Coast tomorrow morning. I scheduled a stopover in Houston just long enough to drop a few things off."

Erin felt a shiver in the sunny room. J.D. was going to fly several hours, rent a car and navigate the crazy Houston interstates for a brief visit. There had to be more to it then he was willing to say on the phone. This must be something he has to do in person.

"I hate to see you go to so much trouble," she tried to dissuade him.

"The itinerary is all set, so don't try to talk me out of it. I have the address and I'll be there by three o'clock."

Yep, the man's on a mission. She prayed it was from God and not Corporate.

Daniel relaxed in his home office on the back side of the second floor, directly above the sun porch. He'd installed an upstairs ringer for the doorbell so he wouldn't miss package deliveries. When the front bell chimed, he glanced up from his discipleship study to the time flashing in the corner of his computer monitor. It was Sunday afternoon and he wasn't expecting anyone.

Must be for Dana.

The bell rang a second time.

"I've got it," he called. Three steps from the bottom of the staircase he saw the visitor through the arched window in the door. Candace Dickerson. The curvy blonde was beyond neighborly, she was downright available.

But in a nice Southern girl way.

Candace was unmarried, educated, produced cooking shows for the local cable station and attended Abundant Harvest. She was everything a red-blooded man in his late thirties would be looking for in a woman and mother for his child. But Daniel wasn't looking. He was content to raise Dana by himself, never dating or accepting invitations to singles' social events. His unattached status suited his daughter just fine and he preferred to keep it that way.

But nothing stopped Candace from trying.

"Hey, Daniel!" She gave his waist a squeeze with one arm and kissed the air near his face as only a proper

Texas gal can. "Your sweet mama said you'd be bringin' company home and I thought I'd drop off a fresh batch of my homemade pecan pralines."

"Did I hear 'pralines'?" Dana called as she hurried down the stairs. The two women hugged and his daughter helped herself to the tin of gooey confections.

"Interesting you heard the mention of candy but you didn't hear the doorbell." Daniel was actually grateful for Dana's arrival. His daughter's presence would keep everything family-friendly.

"Come on out to the porch and meet Erin." Dana led the way.

"Why sure," Candace agreed, looking to Daniel who offered no explanation. She fell into step behind Dana.

Trepidation gripped Daniel anew each time he remembered Erin was in his home, in their lives. She'd gotten comfortable in the rattan chaise near the windows. Her hair was backlit by the setting summer sun casting a rosy halo around her tanned face. She wore some of the loose-fitting gray scrubs Walter Reed tailored to accommodate the physical limitations of their soldiers. They were functional but ugly.

LaVerne relaxed on the matching love seat and something the two just shared had them smiling. Since his mama was prone to telling stories from his days as a boy on the ranch, Daniel had good reason to suspect their amusement was at his expense.

His neighbor passed through the French doors to the sun porch as Dana made the introductions. "Grandma Verne, you already know Candace, right?"

"Yes, hello again," LaVerne greeted the newcomer.

"Nice to see you, Mrs. Stabler." Candace addressed

his mama but her eyes immediately settled on the stranger in the room.

Dana offered her grandmother the open tin, then perched on the edge of the chaise. "And Candace, this is my mother, Erin Gray. You've probably heard of her, because she's a famous photographer."

Erin lowered her chin and closed her eyes for a brief moment. Then she turned a smile of embarrassment toward Candace. "It's nice to meet you, and please excuse Dana's exaggeration. She will be less inclined to brag on me once she figures out most people have no idea who I am."

"They may not know you by name, but you're fooling yourself if you think people don't recognize your work," Daniel insisted.

He reached toward a stack of *National Geographic* magazines, took one from the top and flipped it to a dog-eared page.

"I read where they receive over a million submissions every year. This one made the editor's top pick and then went on to be selected for a global refugee campaign." He was proud of Erin's accomplishments but couldn't help wondering if her accolades could ever make up for their losses. The personal cost of her success had been high for all of them, especially Dana. Daniel's years of praying for the grace to forgive Erin had never been fully fruitful. Constant reminders of their splintered family made it impossible not to know moments of anger, days of regret.

He pushed aside his selfish thoughts and handed the magazine to Candace. Her gaze softened as it brushed the face of an orphan in Darfur. The toddler stood amid the horrifying evidence of genocide.

"Of course I've seen this. How could anyone forget those eyes and that tiny child clinging to her family?" Candace placed the pages in Dana's waiting hand, and then it was her turn to duck her head. "That sure shines a light on the triviality of my cookin' shows."

"Please don't take it that way," Erin insisted. "Your reaction is exactly why I don't like a personal fuss over what I do. People start making comparisons and end up feeling bad instead of being moved to act, which is the point of my work. That picture is just one example of the tragedies I've witnessed in this world. Most folks can never understand loss and abandonment unless they're confronted with it face-to-face."

Dana stood, tossed the magazine to the bed and moved toward the door. "You'd be surprised how much some of us can get our heads around loss and abandonment."

Chapter Four

Dana stomped from the room as Erin's stomach plunged like a runaway roller coaster topping the first hill.

What a tragic choice of words!

From the looks on the faces of Daniel, LaVerne and Candace, they not only read Erin's thoughts, they echoed them.

"Let me see you to the door." LaVerne pushed herself up from the love seat and guided the visitor from the solarium. The pretty blonde knitted together beauty queen brows to show Daniel her concern and then turned her attention to the real power behind the man. His mama.

Daniel closed the French doors after the two women so he could speak privately. While he settled in a nearby armchair, Erin braced herself for the lecture that was sure to come. He arched his back, rubbed both hands through his short-cropped hair, and then leaned toward her with his elbows resting on the knees of his dark-wash jeans.

"Erin, I don't know where to start." His voice was heavy with exasperation.

She held out her left palm and lowered her eyes in defeat. "Daniel, I'll understand if you want to start by packing me off to a local rehab center. Or maybe it would be easier on you if I leave with J.D. when he shows up tomorrow. He can arrange to get me back to New York."

Daniel thrust his chin forward and squinted, angled one ear toward her like he hadn't heard clearly. "You just got here. Why would you want to leave already? And what's this about J.D. coming to Houston?"

"You heard what a stupid thing I just said in front of Dana and you saw how she reacted. It's bad enough that I'm disrupting your lives and keeping your mother away from her ranch. Upsetting Dana like that was never my intention and I don't want everybody walking on egg shells thinking I'll choke on my foot again at any moment."

Daniel slumped back into the chair. He looked more relaxed now.

"Erin, listen to me." A note of understanding mingled with the frustration in his voice. "Dana's a sixteen-year-old girl. She *looks* for reasons to be upset. That's what girls her age do for entertainment. So, don't be too tough on yourself."

"You mean you're not angry with me?"

His forehead wrinkled as if he were pondering the simple question.

"I'm tryin' real hard to keep *angry* from being the right word. Look, I'm a daddy raising a daughter on my own with no help and no game plan other than God's. That's not a complaint, just a statement of fact," he insisted. "Occasionally, I hit a home run but lots of days with that kid are strikeouts. You're gonna have to figure her out for yourself but I'll advise where I can."

"I'm listening," Erin encouraged him to continue.

"For starters, you need to choose your words more carefully when Dana's around. Mostly 'cause she's got a memory like a bear trap and she'll snare you with your own comments when you least expect it. What you just said was insensitive, that's for sure. But it doesn't justify puttin' you out on the street, if that's what you expected. Not tonight, anyway."

The last words were tacked on with humor but there was warning in them just the same.

"Got it." Erin made a mental note. "What else?"

"Oh, there's plenty more but we'll take it as it comes. Mostly be prepared that even though she's agreed not to press you, she has about as much self-restraint as a wolf in a butcher shop. She won't lay back and wait on your lead for long."

"I know." Erin fixed her eyes on the putty in her hand, grateful for the valuable guidance he was giving. "Thank you, Daniel."

"You don't have to keep sayin' that. I know you're out of your element, and for Dana's sake I'll support you whenever I can 'cause it's the right thing to do."

Relief wrapped Erin like the warm blanket LaVerne put over the bed each time she turned down the thermostat. The certainty of Daniel's help was unexpected and comforting, but Erin felt sure his good graces had limits, as well.

"So, what do I do now? I don't have any experience making amends with a teenager."

"Trust me, you're gonna get plenty of practice. I'll go talk to her and I wager you dollars to doughnuts she makes some excuse to come back down. You pray about it in the meanwhile and you'll know what to say when the time comes."

She nodded. The man was kind, supportive and as handsome as any country western star. It was no wonder the pretty neighbor lady was hot on the heels of his fancy boots.

"All right, then." Daniel slapped his palms on the tops of his thighs and leaned forward as if preparing to stand.

"If I could just say one more thing." Erin interrupted his effort to leave. "I owe you for so many reasons, not the least of which is raising Dana in a Christian home. That means a lot."

"I always hoped you'd feel that way. There were times during our few months together when you gave me the impression you had a foundation of faith."

"I did, but it wasn't by design. It was because the foster parents dumped us kids off for vacation Bible school at every church in the area. I'm sure we went to five or six programs each summer. Every home I lived in did the same thing so it seemed like common practice. You didn't have to be very old to figure out it had nothing to do with providing a Christian environment. They were just unloading us for the day."

"Did knowing that bother you?"

"Not after a while. The church volunteers showed us kindness we wouldn't have gotten any other way. And the food was a nice change." She smiled at one of her few pleasant memories of those days. Hot dogs and s'mores always made her think of Jesus. "The summer I was fourteen, I got baptized in a little limestone sanctuary near San Marcos. They gave me a certificate with the date on it but I lost what few keepsakes I had in all the moves. I forgot the name of the church, but I always wondered if it was still there."

"It's pretty easy for me to find out if you really want to know. There's not much I can't dig into."

She felt a razor-sharp point of pain low in her back and winced away from the sensation. Daniel noticed and without a word he was on his feet, moving her efficiently from the chaise to the bed, casually tucking a pillow beneath her knees. He lowered the headboard to shift her weight then pulled the bedclothes over her hospital garb. Lastly, he injected the evening dose of meds into her IV port.

Erin couldn't help but mull over all Daniel had sacrificed and continued to do for her. She knew it was because of what she meant to him as Dana's mother and had nothing whatever to do with who she was as a woman.

And just as well, since it would complicate a situation that was already a big honkin' psychological mess.

Daniel was relieved to see Erin once again comfortable now that he'd settled her on the hospital bed and positioned things as he'd been taught. Following instructions was second nature on the ranch, but his years as a city detective had put him on the giving end of orders. It was good to realize he was not such an old law enforcement dog that he couldn't pick up tricks of a new trade if the situation required it.

"So tell me about J.D. coming for a visit," Daniel recalled her comment.

"He phoned earlier, said he'd made plans to layover in Houston on his way to the West Coast and wants to stop by. He has something for me."

Daniel dropped back into the nearby chair. "J.D. seems like a good man, and I get the impression he doesn't have much downtime. So whatever it is, must be important."

"I just hope it's not a pink slip that has to be delivered in person."

"No way." Daniel scrunched his face at the very idea.

"Well, think about it logically. Most businesses these days are looking for ways to cut costs, not add to them by carrying the salary of a disabled employee on the books. Especially one who may never be able to perform at peak level again."

"And what if you can't, Erin? Would that be such a tragedy? Couldn't you take your experiences and use them in speaking or teaching? You saw how eager Ken was to have you talk to our college-bound students."

The shake of her head was adamant. "I'm not even going to entertain a thought like that, not as a career anyway. One way or the other, I'll get back into the field. If World View doesn't want me, I'll go freelance."

She won't even try. She's still so caught up in running that she can't conceive of an alternative. For all the years that have passed, she really hasn't grown up at all.

A light tapping caused Daniel to turn from his thoughts. Dana was peering through one of the door's dozen panes of glass. Her face sagged with self-pity. He waved her in to join them.

"Hey, darlin' girl. I was heading up to see you right after I got Erin settled and squared away with her meds."

Dana stepped across the threshold but remained near the door. "I'm supposed to help with all that."

"You can do it tomorrow after we whip up a big

breakfast. It'll be an exhausting day for Erin with her therapy starting in the morning and then J.D. coming for a visit in the afternoon."

"When are you going back to work, Dad? Won't the Captain be expecting you soon?"

"I haven't been out of touch, just out of the office. I can get most of my stuff done from here and then go in a couple of times a week to hook up with the team." Daniel reached out, encouraging her to come closer. "Why do you ask? You tryin' to get rid of me?"

"Not even," she admitted shyly as she stepped into the curve of his arm. "Having you around all the time is not so bad."

"Well, that's the nicest thing anybody's said about me all day." A quick squeeze and jostle produced a self-conscious giggle.

Dana pulled free and slipped to the foot of the bed, careful not to bump Erin's legs.

"Can we talk about what happened before?" she addressed her father.

"Do you really want to talk or do you just want to lecture," he teased, having been on the receiving end of many a *talk* with his child.

"Daddy, you're not making this any better." She was as stern as a sixteen-year-old can be with Barney-colored hair, black fingernails and a dozen jangling bracelets.

"Okay, let's hear it." He glanced at Erin who'd been so quiet he thought she might have fallen asleep from the effects of her meds. But her eyes were wide with interest as she spoke up.

"I'd like to be the one to start by apologizing to you,

Dana. I was on my soapbox, all high and mighty about making the world sensitive to the plight of people in other countries. And what I said was insensitive to a person right here in the room. And not just any person, either."

Daniel held his breath, wanting Erin to acknowledge Dana as her daughter but fearful the aftermath would shake his already unsteady turf.

"You're a very insightful girl who understands some of the things I talked about firsthand. And you don't need my photos to show you how it feels. Maybe someday when we know each other better, I'll explain and you can forgive me for forcing you to learn such difficult lessons."

Maybe someday?

Maybe someday Erin would share more when the time was right? Incredibly, his child who always pushed him for an answer seemed to accept Erin's lack of one. His gut churned for his daughter and his pride winced with the unfairness of his position.

He watched as Erin rotated her left wrist, stretching open her fingers. Dana understood. As she slipped her hand into her mother's, she ripped away a small piece of his heart. What could he do but let it go?

"All better?" Daniel asked, speaking casually to disguise his pain.

"Only halfway." Dana turned smudgy dark eyes on him and narrowed them like she was looking down the sight of a weapon. She was the windshield and he was the bug. This was not gonna be good. Dana pointed to the *National Geographic* on the bed. "How can you have that magazine just lying around the house like it's a phone book? How can you treat something so casually when it would be precious to me? And how could you know my mother's whereabouts all this time and still lie to me about her?"

"Now, hold on, little lady." Daniel straightened on the edge of the chair but resisted the urge to jump to his feet, the preferable position a man takes when defending his honor. "I may have withheld the answers to your questions, but I've never lied to you."

"What about the time I asked if you knew what happened after she left us and you said you lost all touch once the custody papers were signed."

"That's true. We never had any further contact."

"Maybe *she* never had any contact with *you,* but you've been keeping track of her career. You've known where she was for years and you never told me."

"Dana, that wasn't his fault," Erin intervened. "Your father is an honorable man. He stuck to the agreement I insisted upon."

"Agreement?" Dana's voice climbed an octave.

"Yes, that's right." Erin took the heat. "At eighteen I was not emotionally capable to care for you, but being a father was what Daniel wanted more than anything. I gave him full custody and he gave me anonymity. I know that sounds cold and businesslike, but we were young and it was the only thing I knew to do. Daniel went along with me and I have thanked God every day for sixteen years that he did."

"Let me get this straight." Dana's voice wavered with youthful indignation. She tugged her fingers but Erin squeezed to maintain the contact. "Having a daughter was so horrible that you ran away."

Erin closed her eyes for long seconds. Daniel

prayed along with her. *Abba Father, if this is the time, give her the words.*

"No, baby. My family background was so horrible that I couldn't risk exposing you to the person I was back then or the conditions I grew up in."

Chapter Five

"When do you think Erin might tell us the rest, Dad?" Dana spoke above the music piped through her ear buds.

She perched on a tall kitchen stool, swirling the ice in her Coke with a plastic straw while Daniel dabbed butter on the top crust of his world-class cobbler. Okay, maybe he'd only competed once against the other men at Abundant Harvest, but he was proud of the blue ribbon taped to the refrigerator door.

He looked first in the direction of the sun porch and then the laundry room before he motioned for his daughter to turn down the volume on her iPod.

"That's up to her," he replied, satisfied they couldn't be overheard. "Erin obviously had a tragic childhood and can't bring herself to talk about whatever happened. And if she wants to keep it that way, you're gonna have to respect her wishes."

Dana nodded. "It must have been a drag growing up in foster homes."

"And she was only a year older than you are right now

when she was out on her own. Erin was on a work-study program at Austin Community College when we met."

He recalled how her eyes had caught his attention when she'd glanced up from a thick volume in the University of Texas library. He was nearly finished with his degree in criminology and she had victim's eyes if ever he'd seen them.

"Did you love her, Daddy?" Dana question was wistful, her amber eyes pleading for affirmation.

"From the first time we met," he admitted, knowing he'd behaved both foolishly and sinfully. And sadly, he'd fallen for a woman who could not return his emotions. "But Erin was just a teenager. She'd already taken so many hard knocks that it was impossible for her to deal with motherhood and marriage."

"Do you think it's possible, now?"

He wiped floury palms on a dish towel, slung it over his shoulder and moved around the granite counter to wrap Dana in his arms for as long as she'd allow it. He pressed a kiss at the edge of her pointy hair.

"Baby girl, don't fool yourself that Erin's gonna stay or even stay close. She has a life on the other side of the world and she's determined to get back to it. Just remember that in a couple more years, you'll go off to college. Then maybe when you're out of school, the two of you will have opportunities to spend time together. But right now, like you kids say, it is what it is."

As expected, Dana ducked from beneath his arm, spun the volume dial on her iPod and grabbed her cell phone off the kitchen counter. Before the patio door closed behind her she muttered "Not till the fat lady sings."

Daniel slid the cobbler into the hot oven and winced

for the hundredth time that morning as a muffled grunt of painful exertion came from the next room. The physical therapist had been with Erin for the past two hours, and she would repeat the visit six out of seven days in the coming weeks.

Having taken a Louisville Slugger to his knee during a gang fight years ago, Daniel knew something of the hard work involved in rehabilitating a limb. Even so, it pained him to hear the grueling regimen of stretches and weight-bearing exercises required for mending a pelvis and a nearly incapacitated arm.

He prayed constantly over the situation knowing God's answer, like the double-edged sword of His Word, could cut both ways. By the end of the summer, somebody in the house was likely to be hurting grievously, whichever way the Father willed.

Erin was nearly breathless but happy to be working her muscles and to finally be free of the IV. "I have never sweated so much this side of Greenwich Mean Time in my life," she panted.

"Your effort vas commendable, Ms. Gray. Keep up zis pace und get plenty of rest between vorkouts and ve have a chance to meet your deadline." Christina's reassuring manner was the only thing that kept her from seeming like a Slavic Terminator.

Erin's limbs were damp and trembling from the morning's labors. The PT in the hospital had been challenging, but it hadn't fully prepared her for today's experience. Christina Heutger was a drill sergeant with a charming accent, hired specifically for her record of producing fast results. The woman would live up to her reputation or kill Erin in the process. Since she was willing to die trying, they were a perfect match.

"I go a little easier on you tomorrow?" Christina offered, wanting her client to decline.

"Don't you dare," Erin wheezed. "There's a G8 meeting in the fall. If I'm not back in Iraq by then, I intend to be at that summit in Japan."

"As you vish." Christina turned away to pack a few items into her duffel, but most of the equipment she brought would remain at the house. "Eat often, conserve energy for our vorkouts and don't play tough by skipping ze pain medication. Cooperate and ve get you on your feet soon."

"Any other instructions, Herr Commandant?" Erin teased as her new friend prepared to leave.

Christina turned back, compassion softening her intense blue eyes and square jaw.

"As a matter of fact, yes, zer is. Ve are in zis togezer, Erin. But even if ve do everyzing in our power correctly, zere is so much to healing zat is outside our control." Christina pointed to the plaque above the window. "So zat is ze most important zing in my opinion."

Erin had already committed the wisdom to memory.

Prayer does not change God, but it changes the one who prays.

"In other words, pray that God changes my will in case I don't change His?"

"Prezactly."

"LaVerne, how long can you afford to stay away from your ranch?" Erin asked.

Her head was bent forward in submission to

LaVerne's blow-drying skills. They were near the end of a string of embarrassing acts that constituted being groomed by another person. But LaVerne didn't seem to mind a bit so Erin went with the flow and covered the awkward moments with conversation.

"Well, that's the beauty of having a married son who lives nearby and works the place. Jake and Becky will have it all to themselves one day and this is good practice for when I go home to be with my Maker."

"Did you always live in West Texas?"

"Goodness, no. I was a city girl. Grew up in Fort Worth and met my Percy when he brought a herd of Angus to the stockyard in '62. As tickled as my mama was to see me married off to a Christian man, she was not too happy about him carrying me almost four hundred miles from home. Even today, the coyotes, rattlesnakes and scorpions give me the willies, but it turned out to be a wonderful place to raise our two sons."

"Does it bother you that Daniel didn't stay in Fort Stockton?"

"It did early on 'cause he's my baby. But from the time Percy took the boys to visit the Texas Ranger museum in Waco till Daniel was commissioned, he never wanted to be anything else. When Jake was ropin' and brandin' fence posts, Daniel had his nose in books about the early days of outlaws and renegades," LaVerne reminisced. "My, how that boy dreamed of wearing the badge."

She tossed the hair dryer into a laundry basket, finger-combed Erin's short bob and pronounced it cute as a bug's ear.

"Daniel's where he always wanted to be and Jake could run the Double-S in his sleep. We only work about three hundred head these days. That's hardly enough cattle for a proper Texas cookout." She chuckled. "Why, we make more money leasing land to mule deer and blue quail hunters than we do selling cows. With close to no rain for the last twenty-something years, everybody's just had to adjust."

"I did a pictorial once on the drought in East Africa. The starvation and disease were horrendous."

"Well, we're not that bad off yet, but all the ranchers are about in the same shape. We're prayin' for another big turnout at the Barbecue Bonanza. Folks all over Texas have to get in their cars and drive out there or we'll never make our goal."

"Why not skip it altogether?" Dana suggested as she entered the room leaving the doors standing wide. She carried what looked like a huge T-shirt the color of red dirt. It had been split open all the way down one side. "Don't do the barbecue this summer. Give people a chance to miss it and then you'll draw an even bigger crowd next year."

"Nothin' doin'. No matter what we have to climb over or run around, the cook-off happens or somebody at the boys' ranch may not get a nice Christmas."

LaVerne accepted the garment and motioned for Erin to raise her left arm. Daniel's mama slipped the shirt over Erin's head and arm, whisked it behind her back and beneath her bandaged right side, finally snapping it shut down the seam.

"There, how's that?" LaVerne stepped back to admire her work. "I probably coulda done better with one of my caftans or even a bed sheet, but Daniel insisted I use this old thing of his."

"I can't believe he actually parted with it, much less let you take a pair of scissors to it," Dana added.

Erin ducked her chin to her chest to see down the length of her body. Even upside down there was no mistaking the Texas Longhorn mascot. Bevo exhaled puffs of smoke and raised his hoof in the Hook 'Em Horns hand signal that even college football fans outside of the Lone Star State generally recognized.

She looked ridiculous in the billowing jersey but she savored the glimmer of a memory it invoked of wearing Daniel's big T-shirts during her pregnancy.

"Dad is gonna crack up when he sees you in that thing."

"In a good way, I hope," Erin joked.

"Oh, for sure. One of these days when you're able to climb the stairs to his office, you can see the rest of his Texas memorabilia." Dana grinned and rolled her eyes.

Erin had no plans to see the second floor of Daniel's home, but now her curious nature buzzed. LaVerne had said something else of interest that called for more detail.

"Tell me more about this barbecue."

"It's lame." Dana's smile disappeared as she crumpled into a chair as if her spine had just collapsed. "And it spoils the last two weeks of my summer every single year."

"Don't listen to that one." LaVerne waved away her grandchild's attitude. "It's a wonderful event to raise funds for the West Texas Boys Ranch. Barbecue champs drag their pits and smokers from all over the country for our three-day rib and brisket competition."

"And Daddy uses me as slave labor."

LaVerne narrowed her eyes and pointed an index finger minus the fake nail at Dana.

"For the eleventy-dozenth time, everybody on the Double-S works, no exceptions. And when you're there, that includes you, princess. It's not a bed and breakfast. It's a working cattle ranch that just happens to sponsor a big event one weekend a year." LaVerne planted both fists on full hips and glared at her grandchild. "And the worst you've ever done is set under a tent in the shade and sell popcorn, so stop your whining or I'll give you something to whine about." She turned to Erin and shielded her mouth as if pretending to be sharing something hush-hush.

"I think I'll put the country cousins in charge of Dana this year and they'll have her muckin' out stalls."

"I am not going to shovel horse droppings!"

"Then stop actin' like the end of the horse that produces 'em."

"Okay, ladies," Daniel called from the kitchen. "As much as I'm enjoying the direction your conversation is going, I'd like to speak with Erin before her guest arrives. So, is everybody decent?"

"Sure, come on in," the women chorused.

Erin glanced at the mantel clock. Two forty-five. Her stomach had only recently stopped quivering from the morning's physical exertion and now it began to quake for a different reason. What could J.D. possibly have that was so important he needed to deliver it in person?

"Wow!" Daniel didn't care that his outburst was loud.

He felt a grin split his face ear to ear. He stopped three steps into the room, pointed at Erin and then tipped his face to the ceiling to howl with amusement. The ladies in the room joined in his infectious laughter.

"Stop," Erin cried as she caught her breath. "It's too painful to laugh that hard!"

"Oh, my stars, that was good." Daniel reigned in the silly behavior, then dragged the heels of his hands across his eyes and cheeks to clear away tears. "I haven't laughed like that since I don't know when."

"Was it worth two hundred and fifty bucks, Dad?"

"Every penny," he assured Dana, touching his finger to his lips to hush her up about the item he'd won at auction.

"What's all that about?" Erin asked.

"Nothing important. May I get a close look at the finished product?" Daniel moved to the bed without waiting for a response. He bent low, reached for the shirt's seam lined with snaps, then turned to nod approval.

"Well done!" He gave his mama kudos. "I can hardly tell it's been cut."

"You said to show Earl Campbell's jersey proper respect, so I did," LaVerne huffed, as if insulted. She propped a laundry basket filled with damp towels and women's hair care stuff on her hip, and motioned for Dana to follow without argument.

"The cobbler's cool if you want a dish," Daniel offered, hoping to sweeten his daughter's disposition and speed up her exit. She was goober-lipped from talking about their annual trip to the Double-S.

That was another logistical matter he had to sort out. They couldn't go off and leave Erin alone in Houston but neither could he let his family down. His brother was hard enough to make peace with on the subject of the day-to-day needs of the ranch. Jake would have a conniption if he thought Daniel might try to beg off at the busiest time of the year.

Daniel settled in a bedside chair, still shaking his head over Erin wearing his prized collectible.

"Cobbler, huh? So that's the smell that's been flirting with my nose for the past couple of hours." Erin sniffed at the air.

"I figured J.D. would appreciate a fresh cup of coffee and something sweet to tide him over till his fancy first-class airline dinner."

"Are you kidding? When you travel on World View's budget, your per diem is the equivalent of a tuna fish sandwich and a bag of chips."

"Really?" Daniel hadn't suspected her employer was so tight with the financial reins. "Then how do you account for the private jet treatment you got on the way out here?"

The medical stupor they put her in for travel must have done the trick because she appeared to be considering that cost for the first time.

"I don't know." Erin seemed puzzled. "I'll have to ask J.D. about the funding."

The doorbell chimed.

"I think you're fixin' to get the opportunity." Daniel stood and turned to get the door.

"Wait! Move me to the chaise before you let him in. Please, Daniel," she pleaded. "He needs to see me out of a hospital bed. And if J.D. *is* here to fire me, then at least let me take the news in a vertical position."

The bell chimed again.

"Just a moment," Daniel called toward the foyer. He moved to Erin's side, scooped her up and deposited her on the chair by the windows. But before he pulled away, he gave himself the simple pleasure of enjoying her fresh scent.

The smell was womanly and inviting. To cover the inappropriate thought, he tossed his favorite old handmade blanket over Erin's legs and hurried away.

"Welcome, my friend." Daniel swung the front door wide as he greeted J.D. "Here, let me help you with those things."

The casually dressed man on the porch carried two large boxes in his arms, one stacked atop the other. Daniel relieved J.D. of the cartons, surprised by their weight.

"What's in here, bricks?" Daniel asked.

"Just a few trinkets for Erin," J.D. replied.

"She's out here on the sun porch." Daniel stepped to the side and let Erin's boss enter.

A look of affection spread across J.D.'s face the moment he spotted her on the chaise.

"Look at you." J.D. was obviously pleased. "Out of that bed and wearing something besides those jerry-rigged hospital scrubs."

She held out her left arm to show off the jersey and accept a gentle hug.

"I have my host to thank on both counts."

Daniel was humbled by the credit she continually gave him. He lowered both boxes to the floor, motioned for J.D. to take a seat and then dragged up a side chair for himself.

"So, all my worry that you were languishing in this humid heat, pining for the deserts of the Middle East was a waste of energy, huh?" J.D. settled on the love seat.

"I admit the humidity is a nice change for my dry skin and I certainly don't miss the grit in my food. But I'm on the recovery fast track. I'll be at the fall G8 if I'm not already back in the field."

Daniel's heart thumped at the news and J.D.'s brows shot toward his thinning hairline.

"Erin, that's very aggressive. Why don't we just take it one step at a time and talk about assignments in a few months."

"Because this isn't going to take a few months. Look, I'm in otherwise perfect health and following all the doctor's instructions. I refuse to let this *inconvenience* get the best of me." She raised her right elbow to show off her ability to wiggle her thumb. "I'm only down for a little while. Please, don't count me out."

"Kid, you can't put a recovery like this on a timeline and expect your body to comply. I'm afraid you're setting yourself up for failure with such high expectations."

"It's not *expectations,* J.D.! It's my strategy to get my life back on track!" For a moment Daniel thought she might burst into tears. But as quickly as her anxiety surfaced, calm returned to Erin accompanied by a loud exhale. "My work is the only thing I know. It's all I've got and you can't take it away from me now."

Daniel understood the importance of work. His position with the Rangers was one he'd prized since childhood. Still, in his heart he knew his family was what mattered most. His work could disappear tomorrow and he'd be fine. Only a threat to his child could cause him to relate to the panic Erin was feeling. Would she ever be capable of showing the mother's love Dana craved? And if the answer to that question was no, why didn't that make him feel better?

Chapter Six

Daniel remained quiet, keeping his thoughts to himself. He'd known Erin was bound to plead her case with J.D., but witnessing the emotionally charged comments made him feel like an eavesdropper. He stood, prepared to leave and give them privacy.

"You don't need to go." Erin read his intentions. "This is your home and you have every right to know I'm doing my part to get better so we can all move on with our lives."

Confusion was not a familiar state for Daniel. He weighed the facts, called the shots, took action and moved on. Most days that strategy was easier with a team of Texas Rangers than with a teenage girl, but he'd always managed.

Until now.

Whichever way he looked at it, this situation with Erin was a no-win wrapped up in a heartache. There was so much on the line. But each time he thought he knew the worst that could happen, she did something kind or said something endearing to ratchet up the stakes.

His child was bursting with the pride of finding her

mama, of discovering Erin's accomplishments. Dana's psychological void of not knowing the other half of her heritage was slowly shrinking thanks to the few jigsaw pieces Erin was willing to supply. And even if she hadn't come into their lives by choice, the comfort Dana had discovered from having Erin in their home was a treasure. Once she was gone, he would be a sorry consolation prize.

Then there was LaVerne, happy as a gopher in soft dirt over having a house in the city to run for a while. Though the widow Stabler was highly respected in her small community, she still drove her big Cadillac to Fort Worth or Houston every chance she got. Being valued for something other than her ability to halter a stubborn bull was like a tonic to his bossy mama. Her laughter on the sun porch was frequent as she enjoyed being appreciated by their female company.

And was it any wonder? At only thirty-four, Erin was a gifted photographer who had traveled the globe, had seen more of life than most people could ever imagine and had been awarded some of the world's highest honors for her work. Daniel was not immune to the impressive allure of Erin Gray and her talent. The few nights she'd been under his roof he'd slept fitfully. Even crept down the stairs in the dark once to confirm it wasn't his imagination.

This Erin might be different from the young woman who'd stood before the justice of the peace with him, but even so when Daniel looked into her eyes during moments of silence, a glimmer of that skittish girl still existed.

He knew her fears, knew her past and knew she would run to catch up with her future as soon as she got the chance.

And that was exactly what he wanted. Right?

* * *

Erin watched Daniel's face and waited. He'd been standing there for several long seconds, not saying a word. She needed his help convincing J.D. to give her another chance. Daniel took his seat again on the thick cushion of the ladder-back chair. He pressed his lips tight for a moment, then released the comment he seemed to be holding back.

"Actually, I agree with J.D. that you're putting too much pressure on yourself."

"What?" She looked from one man to the other. "Is this a conspiracy?"

He raised a palm in defense so she let him continue.

"I agree that you're healing remarkably well and your therapist said you gave a gutsy effort this morning. But this self-imposed deadline could cause the very setback you need to avoid."

She squeezed her eyes shut and opened them again, glancing back and forth, suspicious of where this conversation was headed. She'd never been encouraged by anybody to slow down. Not ever. She lived in a hurry-up world and if she had to lay back and wait much longer, her brain would atrophy along with her muscles.

J.D. leaned close enough to rest a warm palm on her shoulder. "This is not about your employment, Erin. I promise a new passport will be waiting at World View headquarters when you're ready to return."

"But until then, I'm fired, right?"

He stood, pressed his fists into the small of his back and arched forward, muttering about her "hard head" while stretching as he always did after sitting too long.

"As appealing as that sounds to me at the moment,

dismissing you is not why I extended my day by five hours to have this twenty-minute discussion."

"Then what was so important to bring you all the way to Houston?"

J.D. picked up one of the boxes and set it on a nearby end table. Daniel produced a small pocketknife to slit the packing tape. As the ends unfolded, J.D. brushed away foam peanuts and withdrew a leather case bearing a familiar black on yellow logo.

"Oh, J.D., you are the best boss ever and I love you!" She fumbled one-handed with the snaps on the flip-top case. It sprung open dumping a new Nikon digital into her lap. She lifted the camera close to her face and studied it, feeling the knot of uncertainty in her stomach begin to subside for the first time in days.

"What else is in the box?" She craned her neck, eager to see the accessories.

"Oh, just an assortment of lenses, some hardware for downloading and printing and a new laptop, since yours was nearly destroyed in Kirkuk. The IT guys saved what they could of your hard drive."

She looked down at the expensive new camera in her hand and blinked hard several times. She'd lost more than mobility and a laptop when that bomb had exploded. She'd lost three young comrades.

"Thank you," she whispered, grateful yet again to have survived. Then looking up into the faces of J.D. and Daniel, she said it louder. "Thank you both, so much."

"It's a pleasure and the bureau's small way of encouraging your recovery. But that's not even the best part, at least in my humble opinion."

J.D. slit open the second carton, folded back the flaps

and set it on the floor at her left side. Beneath a layer of packing bubbles was a thick mound of envelopes addressed to World View in New York.

"Is this all my junk mail?" she asked, puzzled why he'd bother to haul it all the way to Houston.

"Erin, it is *fan* mail. You know, those handwritten things from people who admire your work?" he teased. "And some of the stories are so incredibly well-written, they will take your breath away."

"You've read them?"

"Well, most of them were generally posted to World View and as soon as the mail room found mention of your name, they sent them to me. There are others addressed to you personally. Of course, they've never been opened."

She sifted through the envelopes noticing the postmarked locations and dates. "Some of these are pretty old."

"I've been telling you for years they were piling up. Since your injuries made headlines at World View, we've had a flurry of new additions to your mail tub. I thought now might be a good time for you to check them out."

There couldn't possibly be anything of interest among the envelopes, some yellowed and dusty and others crisp with recent postmarks. But she appreciated J.D.'s intentions. She reached for a tissue to clean the dust from her hand, then extended it along with her best smile to her boss.

"You were so thoughtful to go to all this trouble. I really mean it."

Instead of taking her hand he glanced around, looking for something.

"Oh, wait." He held up a finger and moved toward

the foyer. "There's more," he called from around the corner. The front door opened, closed almost immediately and then he was back holding the handle of a familiar two-by-three-foot flat binder.

"My portfolio!"

Daniel threw his hands over his ears, an exaggerated reaction to her shriek of excitement.

"Where did you get it?" She reached out to accept the black nylon handle that had traveled what seemed like a million miles slung over her shoulder. "I thought I'd lost it years ago."

"You left it in my office before you took off for Camp Justice and Saddam's execution. I slid it behind a credenza to keep it from getting bent and only ran across it the other day. I had a feeling you'd be happy to have it back." J.D.'s broad smile said he was pleased with himself.

She ran her hand over the worn black case made of faux leather. It represented a time when she couldn't afford anything more. Once she had the money for a nicer portfolio, she wouldn't part with this piece of her history.

"Do you need some help unzipping it?" Daniel offered.

"Not right now." She wasn't ready to share the images hidden inside the binder. Not all of her work had been worthy of prizes. And some of the photos were private, for her eyes only. "Maybe one evening this week, after dinner."

"Speaking of food, how does peach cobbler sound to you?"

Bless him, Daniel had sensed her hesitation and steered the conversation to a sweet subject.

"With ice cream?" J.D.'s bushy brows shot up.

"And fresh coffee," Daniel tempted.

"I'm in! That puny snack they gave me on the flight is long gone."

"J.D., Daniel asked me something earlier that I couldn't answer. Did World View pay for the chartered jet that brought me to Houston?"

"Good grief, no."

"Well, if the company didn't, how was it funded?"

"It was an anonymous gift from someone at Walter Reed who appreciates your talent and wanted to help you."

Erin felt a headache begin to throb as she strained to think of anyone she knew with the kind of money it took to give such an expensive gift.

"I don't understand." She shook her head, stunned by such generosity.

"Well, maybe you're not supposed to. I've been trying to convince you that you have loyal fans. Perhaps now you'll believe it."

"Where's Dana been all day?" Erin inquired as credits for the classic film rolled up the screen.

LaVerne snapped off the television and handed over the remote. "Down at Abundant Harvest with her friends. They're rehearsing for the youth concert, but we're trying to stay away from that sore subject."

"How come?"

"It's always scheduled for the same week as the Double-S cook-off. Poor kid works long hours at the church all summer and then misses the big event."

"Why doesn't Daniel let her stay home?"

"That's another sore subject, but I happen to agree with him on this one. Daniel's a family man. He spends his vacation time at the ranch with us. He's always put family first and he's raised Dana to respect that. The only selfish thing my baby boy ever did was follow his professional dream, and that seed was planted and fertilized by his own daddy. My oldest enjoys giving his brother a hard time about bailing on the family business, but even Jake grudgingly admits that Daniel was never suited for ranching."

"So, if I understand this correctly, Daniel spends his time off from work doing stuff he's not particularly good at and makes Dana go along with him?"

LaVerne's puckered lips and nearly closed eyes said she was considering the statement, but then she shook her blond updo in disagreement.

"No, that's not it. He might would like to spend a week fishin' in Mexico and Dana moans and groans something fierce about the long drive and the hard work. But when the contestants show up and the fun starts, there's no mistaking that the two of them wouldn't miss it for the world. And there's another reason Daniel makes her go."

"He doesn't trust her to stay behind in Houston alone?"

LaVerne chuckled at the thought. "There's probably some truth to that, but it's more about exposing Dana to the people and the place she came from. That girl's been a living game of Twenty Questions since she was old enough to talk. And the more Daniel refused to tell her about you, the more she was determined to be different from him. I swear, the day she discovered Miss Clairol I thought her daddy would have a stroke. She went into the bathroom a pretty girl with shoulder-length auburn hair and came out lookin' like the raven-haired, white-faced offspring of that Manson fellow."

"Charles?"

"No! Marilyn!"

"She doesn't look that drastic now, so her taste must have moved back toward the center."

"That's thanks to Daniel. Once he came down off the ceiling, he decided to play it cool. Acted like it was no big deal. He said as long as she wasn't doing anything illegal or immoral, it was her choice to go to school lookin' like a freak every day."

"Well, his plan seemed to have worked."

"Don't be fooled by the way she's dressed today. Tomorrow it may be Gap jeans and a polo shirt. She's reinvented herself more times than Madonna."

Erin was learning a lot from the chatty older woman. "I'm impressed, LaVerne. You know pop culture."

"Hey, we have a satellite dish! I may have been raised on Elvis but every now and again I have an MTV moment."

While LaVerne picked up their dessert dishes and carried them to the kitchen sink, Erin considered this latest news. One thing was abundantly clear. Daniel's primary motivation for her presence in his home was to give Dana a better sense of self. The girl was obligated to spend time with her daddy's family whether she related well to them or not. She deserved equal time with her mother to balance the country connection. But what if the nature of Erin's family trumped the nurture of Daniel's? Wouldn't that do Dana more harm than good?

"Can I get some of this packing stuff out of your way?" LaVerne was back and referring to the boxes J.D. had brought.

"Don't bother with that heavy carton. I'll get Dana to help me unpack and inventory everything tomorrow.

But if you wouldn't mind taking care of the other box, that would be nice."

"You want me to sort these letters and stack 'em where you can reach 'em?"

"No, just tape the box closed and store it in the garage."

LaVerne looked at Erin like she'd just said a dirty word. "You can't just put these people back on the shelf like spare parts. They spent a lot of time putting their thoughts on paper for you. It would be disrespectful to ignore what they have to say."

"If you feel that strongly, then why don't you look through them for me, LaVerne?"

"Really?" Her brows lifted as she considered the offer. "You wouldn't think it was an invasion of your privacy?"

"Of course not, you'd be doing me a favor. Besides, there's nothing private about a communication from someone I don't know."

LaVerne stooped to grasp the box and with an "Ooof" of exertion, realized it was too bulky for her to manage.

"Well, thanks. These will be good company between my soaps for the next couple of weeks. Then we go back to the ranch, and the million-and-one details of the cook-off."

"Hopefully by then I can manage on my own, or maybe Christina would be willing to stay here with me."

"I'm not leaving you behind. You're coming home with us." The response was as matter-of-fact as it was unexpected. "I'll put you to work just like I do every-body. Why, you can be our official photographer!"

"Is that a job offer or an invitation?" It sounded like a genuine reason to get comfortable with her new equipment.

"It's whatever you want it to be, Erin. You're part of our family for as long as it suits you. Family never needs an invitation at my place."

Chills of skepticism gave Erin a shiver. "What do you think Daniel will have to say about that?"

"Say about what?" Daniel stood in the doorway, all six foot two of him looking every bit the Texas Ranger from the soles of his black cherry boots to the crown of his wheat-colored cowboy hat.

Chapter Seven

"I was just tellin' Erin that she'll be goin' out to the Double-S with us for the festivities."

Daniel removed his Stetson and held it at his waist poised above his silver buckle. He studied his hatband while he considered the awkward situation his mama had just created. The sudden racing of his heart told him it was either a dreadful idea or an answer to prayer.

"Yep," LaVerne continued, "I told her we'd be puttin' her to work, too. Everybody pulls their own weight on a ranch and even if she can only pull with one hand, every little bit helps."

"That's a fact," he went along as if he hadn't been caught off guard by the conversation. Looking to Erin, he explained. "I handle the stock to free up Jake so he can manage the fund-raiser. Dana's my number one sidekick until the crowd shows for the judging and then we put her in a booth selling cotton candy and cold drinks."

"You know what?" His mama held up her index finger as if she'd just had an epiphany. "If Erin can figure out how to use that fancy new camera, maybe this year instead of a shoe box full of snapshots we'll have a professional album."

"That's a dandy idea, Mama."

"Thank you, son. You think she'll go for it?"

"Excuse me, you two," Erin interrupted their mutual admiration society meeting. "I'm sitting right here."

"So you are." Daniel nodded. "And when I walked in you wanted to know what I had to say about something. What was it, again?"

Erin looked to LaVerne who shrugged. "Hey, answer the man. You just pointed out that you're sittin' right there and I've got laundry to do."

As his mama passed through the double doors she turned back and pointed toward the carton of letters. "Would you mind puttin' that box in my bedroom, please?"

"I'll get it for you in a minute," he agreed. When they were alone, Daniel took a chair near Erin. "What's up?"

Her gaze fixed on the exposed fingertips of her right hand. She worked her ball of putty, carefully pressing with first one digit and then another, killing time.

"Something make you uncomfortable?" He waited until her lovely eyes finally met his.

"Your mother's invitation was rather sudden and I wasn't sure you approved of her extending it to me."

He rested against the back of the chair as he pondered how to make the best of the circumstances. Might as well be honest. "I'll admit this is news to me, but I can see where it could kill two birds with one stone. I can't beg off the trip but I don't want to leave you here alone, either. If you'll agree to come to the ranch, that'll give you and Dana more time together and we can all continue helping with your therapy."

"But won't it send the wrong message?" Erin asked.

"And what message would that be?"

"That I'm somehow to be welcomed with open arms when the fact is I bailed out on you and Dana years ago?"

"Well, here's the deal. In that respect, you'll be in good company because that's basically the way my brother feels about me. Jake passes cheap shots off as jokes but his sentiments are not exactly covert. He interprets my choosing a career over ranching as forsakin' the family. It doesn't matter to him that Daddy supported my choice or that Mama will leave the ranch to Jake. He only sees it one way. His little brother let him down."

A shadow of sadness crossed Erin's face. "So you go back every year to pay your penance?"

"I wouldn't call it that. It's my home, too. I love workin' with the animals and being with my daddy's people. For a little while, anyway. By the end of the visit, I'm usually as eager as Dana to get back to Houston." He smiled at the confession. "This is really where both of us fit in best."

"Won't my being out there make the situation more difficult?"

"It might create a little heat for me, but I'm up to it. And where Dana's concerned, your presence might actually make it better. With you there she'll finally have some braggin' rights over her cousins."

Erin lowered her eyes and shook her head, dismissing his comment.

"Oh, knock off the humble act, will ya, Erin?" The brittle edge to his voice took Daniel by surprise. From the way her jaw sagged, it had the same effect on Erin. But the muscles in his solar plexus were perpetually sore from holding his breath. From holding back bitter words that wanted to escape.

He passed a hand over his eyes, ran it the length of his face and rested it over his lips, too late to catch the biting comment.

"I'm sorry," he muttered. "That was uncalled for."

"But you said it, so it must be what you think."

He stood, crossed the room to stand with his back to her and looked out at the patio he'd built for family meals that would probably never take place.

"Go ahead," she insisted. "Get it off your chest."

He turned, expecting a challenge in her eyes. Instead there was compassion, almost apology. She was willing to accept more verbal blows. After sixteen years of faithfulness, hadn't he earned the right to deliver them?

"I couldn't compete with you as a phantom, Erin. I sure can't measure up to the real deal. You may not feel comfortable basking in the spotlight, but you *are* something of a celebrity. I would really appreciate it if you'd stop waving away your success like it doesn't matter. Because if your accomplishments aren't important, what does that say to Dana about mine?"

"Understood." Erin knew the one-word response was enough.

She didn't dare insult him with an argument. How could a man with the self-confidence to wear that famous star on his chest understand being inferior no matter what your reputation said about you? Yes, she was known for taking chances but there was no risk involved when you had nothing to lose. For some people it came naturally to accept accolades. For her it was like perpetuating a lie.

She had earned the brand of *coward,* but she strove not to be a liar, too.

And now, as she was slowly discovering, though Daniel had been the steadfast, loving parent while she'd fled all responsibility, he seemed to feel he had something to prove. Had this time together become a competition for Dana's respect?

A parental smack down?

No way. Before Erin even got started, she knew the losing end would be hers. Even so, Daniel had allowed her into their home for a specific purpose. She resolved to take the energy she was giving to physical therapy and make the same effort with Dana. Erin would make up for lost time and pray the questioning eyes of her daughter never became the accusing eyes of her sister.

"Understood," she repeated. "I'll be more considerate."

Daniel sunk back into a chair and nudged the carton with the toe of his boot.

"Why does Mama want this in her room?"

What now? If Erin admitted instructing LaVerne to pack away the letters it would fuel Daniel's argument.

"I asked her to sort through them for me." So much for trying not to lie, but she needed a quick cover-up.

"Seriously?" He leaned forward in his chair, his forehead creased with concern.

"I haven't wanted to worry anybody, but my vision blurs occasionally. So, I told LaVerne it was fine with me if she read them." *Forgive me, Lord! I am such a jerk!*

"Hey, I was wrong to spout off like that." He sounded sincere. "You're the one who's had the props kicked out from under you and here I am whining a 'What about me?' tune that I wouldn't abide in anybody else."

"Don't take it back, Daniel. You deserve to have your say and if there's more on your mind, I wish you wouldn't keep it to yourself."

"There's always plenty on my mind, but right now it's mostly work-related."

"Anything you can tell me about? I'm used to more excitement than the value of the big showcase on *The Price is Right.*"

His smile returned, warming her face. "Mama been spending too much time in here?"

"LaVerne's great company. But I've been ducking M-16 fire for a few years now. I'm starving for some intense mental stimulation."

His lips pressed together in concentration, as if he were considering how much to say. After a moment he seemed to relax. With his elbows propped on the armrests, Daniel laced long fingers across his chest.

"I guess there's no harm in telling you about the case as long as you don't share it with Mama or Dana."

"That's okay," she declined. "I don't want you to break any rules of confidentiality just to entertain an adrenaline junkie."

"Oh, no. It's nothing like that. It's just I've always made it a practice to keep the risks of the job to myself so they won't worry about me."

"Daniel, you're a Texas Ranger. Anybody who's heard the name understands what kind of danger comes with that territory."

"Still, I'd rather not bring the particulars home with me. So it's just between us, deal?"

"Deal."

Daniel detailed his team's investigation into an organized effort by an international moving company to bring illegals across the Texas border. Mexican citizens forfeited their life savings only to be loaded and trapped like cargo without proper ventilation, water or food.

News of the human trafficking and the deadly outcome was known nationwide. Even so, the criminals had no problem filling truck after truck with people desperate to escape poverty for the hope of a better life.

"We've finally got an airtight link to three cases. It's close to home and falls under my jurisdiction. With things heating up, I may have to leave at a moment's notice."

"I'm envious." Her gaze fell to the bandages. Few remained wrapped tightly to her body compared to a week ago, and she was happy to be rid of the constant companionship of the IV pole. Still, there was no debating her limited capacity. "Yep, downright jealous that I'm not in a position for a ride-along."

"You know, until this moment I never really thought about how much we have in common professionally."

"Yeah," she nodded, understanding. "We're both strangely exhilarated around bad guys with automatic weapons. Of course, whereas you actually confront them, I'm able to keep mine confined to the space of a viewfinder."

He cocked an eyebrow and looked her up and down before replying, "All evidence to the contrary."

She dipped her chin and shook her head. "You get

ambushed by one little truck bomb and they never let you hear the end of it."

As they shared companionable laughter over the absurd truth of the statement, LaVerne appeared in the doorway.

"Pardon me for interrupting the party, but it's been half an hour since you said you'd bring me that box." She pointed to the carton full of letters.

Daniel hopped to his feet. "Sorry, Mama. I'll do it right now." He hoisted the container to his shoulder and headed for the main floor's master suite.

"LaVerne," Erin called. "Thank you for offering to preview the letters and sort them for me." She gave the older woman an exaggerated wink.

"Preview and sort?" LaVerne's farm-weathered face scrunched like a dried fig.

"Yes, by date or subject. Whichever you choose will be fine with me," Erin insisted, with another staged wink and a jerk of her head toward Daniel's back. "It's really kind of you to do that so I don't strain my eyes."

"Eye strain." She nodded. "Yeeeees, I see said the blind man." The sharp old woman winked back, gave a thumbs-up, and then followed her son toward the hallway.

Erin noted the date on the wall calendar. It was Friday and she'd just been declared the most motivated client Christina had ever *vorked vith.* And now with five days of the brutal therapy behind her, Erin was feeling every inch a survivor. Stronger, more confident of reaching her recovery goal. In spite of Daniel's and J.D.'s cautions, she was making steady progress and even Christina admitted that though very aggressive, the deadline was doable.

Knowing the days were numbered, Erin began to

focus on maximizing her hours with Dana but limiting her time around Daniel. Surely centering her interest on the teen and steering clear of anything that might challenge Daniel would make him feel less threatened, especially as they prepared to head west.

So, in lieu of family dining, Erin invited Dana to share meals in the solarium, ostensibly to rest and conserve strength for each day's workout. Nobody who was in the house during the sessions with Christina would question the logic that coincidentally created an atmosphere for *girl talk*, a language more foreign to Erin than Mandarin.

LaVerne grumbled about having dishes and crumbs strewn around the house. But she seemed otherwise happy to bustle about the solarium delivering, collecting and tidying up, undeterred when most of the conversations between Erin and Dana were on subjects beyond an old woman's ken.

Erin laid aside her Nikon owner's manual one evening when Dana expressed interest in a board game. The teen made a noisy fuss, chanting a challenge to her dad as she climbed the stairs to get the Scrabble box. Erin's face burned with guilt when Dana dragged a card table and three folding chairs into the room, determined her dad would not be excluded. Even as she concentrated on observing the rules, Erin struggled not to laugh at the silly comments Daniel used to distract his opponents or soften the blow of a high scoring win. Though he continually poked at Erin's serious demeanor, the simple fun got under her skin, at least for the one night.

Mornings and afternoons, Daniel knocked and poked his head through the crack in the two doors to see if she needed anything. Each visit she mustered up a bright smile and a "No, but thanks" response, hoping he wouldn't be suspicious that she wasn't asking for his help in moving from one position to the next. Erin wasn't about to display the mobility she'd regained over the hard hours of work. Her progress was a winning hand to be held close to the vest. As long as nobody suspected her game, there would be no pressure on Erin to show her cards.

There was another reason, a more important reason, that Erin was determined to hold something back. As she practiced skin and dental care left-handed before the mirror one morning, the truth of it shocked her to the core. In the cozy bathroom that had become her private space, she was feeling…*at ease*. And on the family porch where Dana joined Erin to watch the summer sun fade, she recognized there was a sense of *belonging*. Even with her efforts to keep a distance, the place and the people had become far too friendly and homey. But like a family scene in a Rockwell painting, those emotions were as weak as watercolor and would dissolve just as easily.

Erin prayed for the strength to avoid the comfortable distractions. Prayed to God that she'd stay the course, work her plan. And that she could hurry back to the uncomplicated life she'd crafted from the wreckage of her childhood without leaving a legacy of damage to her own child.

And she was on track until she made the mistake of showing Daniel her private portfolio.

Chapter Eight

"Is there a particular reason you've been avoiding me all week?"

Erin lowered the old copy of *Time* magazine to find Daniel inside the doorway. Her breathing stilled as she took in how handsome he was in a simple white T-shirt, worn jeans and stocking feet. In this casual state, he was the young man who'd stolen her heart in the library the night they'd met.

It had been as difficult to leave the circle of his arms as to leave behind her tiny baby girl. But as the infant had howled constantly in a language without translation, Erin had recognized the familiar hammering of her heart and pounding in her head. They were the same physical reactions she'd experienced during her father's fits of violence. She was too old to hide anymore. She had to run.

She swallowed past the guilt that was a constant dryness in her throat. There was no point bothering with a smoke screen answer to Daniel's question. Besides, he deserved better.

"We were acting too much like a cozy little family," she admitted.

"Was that so bad?" Daniel made himself comfortable on the foot of the rented bed a few feet from where Erin reclined on the rattan chaise. He spotted minor changes in the room, the juxtaposition of small items that Erin herself had likely moved. She hadn't asked for his help in days, clearly managing on her own.

"No, it wasn't so bad. But the side effects will be."

As much as he hated it, he understood. Still, he made her explain.

"For example?"

She closed the magazine and dropped it to her lap. A curve tugged at his mouth as he caught full view of the football memorabilia he'd sacrificed as a replacement for her dowdy hospital attire.

She spotted his smile and understood the cause.

"I know. I love it, too."

He noted the ease with which she extended both arms away from her body now that she could be free of the sling for a few hours each day.

"Where did you get this big thing, anyway?"

"Don't change the subject. You were about to give me an example of why cozy is bad."

"Daniel, this is a short-term deal," she reminded him. "I'm here a few weeks at best, but it only took a day or two of this make-believe family atmosphere to cause Dana to forget that. Even LaVerne treats me like a reformed prodigal. I won't repay your kindness by creating false expectations any more than I'd steal your silver candlesticks." Her honesty was jarring.

"On the plus side," Erin continued, "Dana knows who I am now. Though we keep our conversations in the present tense, I've been very open about my life and my job. So some of those big questions in her mind should be settled, right? She says she understands the demands of my work and I know high school is a busy time, so I'll leave the future up to her. With the way things are between us today, I can go back to my life without leaving too much upheaval in yours."

He cringed inwardly and blinked at her matter-of-fact manner. She seemed to make sense, though he didn't know whether to admire or despise her sensibility. But no matter how Erin rationalized her developing relationship with her daughter, Dana would not be satisfied knowing her mama through photograph bylines and holiday greetings. His butter bean had been negotiating since she was six. When she went door-to-door collecting for charity, Dana didn't ask whether or not the neighbor would like to donate. She was so sure of closing the deal that she simply asked how much they wanted to give.

There was only one subject where she'd fallen short of success and that was in getting him to talk about her mother. Now that Erin was in the picture, Dana was blossoming in ways he'd never imagined. It would be wrong to expect her to squelch such growth. A shudder threatened as Daniel considered the ultimate impact these few weeks would have on the rest of his life.

"And what about you, Erin?" He shifted attention away from his personal worries.

"What about me?" She snuggled against the pillows

of her chair in a way that would have brought on a yelp of pain a week earlier.

"Has this time with us upset your life?"

"Only in a positive way." As she seemed to consider his question further, she drummed fingertips on the magazine in her lap. Daniel knew from the front cover that Erin's work in Rwanda was featured inside the pages.

"I figured this bum arm would end my career, but Christina assures me it's coming along well. And even if I don't regain full mobility, I've discovered my left hand deserves more credit than I ever gave it before."

She patted her tummy. "I'm not missing any meals and my toenails are back under control." She wiggled bare toes showing off a fresh coat of red polish. "And today I shot and downloaded photos entirely with my left hand."

He mirrored her happy smile, grateful Erin's confidence was returning even if it would only accelerate losing her again from Dana's life. And from his.

"If you'll hand me the computer, I'll show you some great shots of a squirrel scavenging your bird feeder."

He stood, stretched his long legs and reached for her laptop. On the floor, beneath the glass surface of the sofa table, laid the large black case J.D. had brought during his visit. Daniel grabbed the portfolio.

"How about you show me what's in here, instead?"

She wrinkled her nose like he was waving old gym socks. "You'll be disappointed. It's just my personal stuff and none of it has ever seen the light of day," she was apologetic but at least she didn't refuse.

He pulled a chair alongside, swept open the zipper and placed the closed case across Erin's lap. She lifted the cover and let it fall aside, like pulling the opening night curtain of a Broadway show. Daniel watched as her hands reverently touched the enlarged photographs. Her fingers hovered protectively over the images like a new mother blocking the rays of the sun from her infant. His gaze moved to Erin's face where she made no effort to hide angular creases of sadness or smooth waves of satisfaction as she viewed her work.

If he had to guess, he'd say these particular photographs were the very embodiment of her spirit. His heart softened at the raw emotion in her eyes.

"This is the picture that started my obsession." She tilted the book for him to see more clearly.

A horrific two-vehicle head-on accident was spread across the page in hues of black, white and gray. Mangled metal and shards of glass littered an intersection and blocked oncoming traffic. Dark-skinned passersby in light cotton tunics and sandals crowded the sidewalk, astonished stares on their faces. Both drivers were trapped, open eyes unseeing, gone to the life beyond. And in the midst of the devastation was a plump-cheeked toddler strapped into a car seat thrown free of the carnage. She sucked her thumb contentedly, round eyes watching strange faces, not a single curl on her head or lace ruffle of her dress disturbed.

"I was in Pakistan to photograph young Muslims in training to fight the Taliban. This is a major street in Islamabad where a protest against the military was expected. I was ready with my camera when the crash happened only yards from where I was positioned. I got this shot seconds before the baby was scooped up by an emergency worker."

"That child's survival was nothing short of a miracle."

Erin lifted her face, her wide eyes sought his.

"Exactly. But my timing was off. I caught the result of a miracle but missed the act."

"What?" She lost him.

"Look, here's another one." She turned clear page protectors, each one containing a stunning image. "This was a mud slide in Thailand. I shot it through the back window of our bus as it took out the road behind us. I heard it crashing through the trees above us but I missed it."

"If you'd been any closer it wouldn't have missed you!" And Daniel thought *he'd* flirted with death on a few occasions.

She flipped more pages, searching. "Here it is! This time I thought I had it for sure, but when it was developed I was heartsick."

A barefoot Nigerian runner broke the tape of a marathon finish line, his shining face thrown back in glory and agony.

"What was there to be upset about? That guy was a long shot and his record-breaking time was all over the news. You got an incredible picture of his win."

"You don't understand." She shook her head. "I was right there but I still couldn't catch it. At the very moment when he turned his face to the sun, there was an arc of gold over his head. It was like God's blessing settling on the runner. I felt certain that was my moment, but I was wrong."

"Your moment?"

She expelled a deep sigh and closed the case. "That's why I never show this work to anybody. It's completely selfish. It's not about the subjects. It's about me trying to capture a miracle on film."

"Why?"

She ducked her head. "It's embarrassing to admit something so trivial."

"Erin?" Daniel said her name softly, encouraging her as he would Dana. "If it's that important to you, it's not trivial at all."

Her gaze sought his, the need for understanding in the squint of her eyes. After long moments she spoke with reluctance but honesty.

"I want something uniquely my own that I can be proud of, Daniel. Something rare to replace what I missed as a child and gave up as a woman. I need visible proof my life got back on the right track even though it started off so badly."

"Erin, every one of these shots is a testament to that fact."

"But they're incomplete," she insisted.

Incomplete. Like Erin.

Daniel recognized a window of opportunity when the Father opened one. She was in a desperate search for evidence that the evil she'd experienced as a child had been used for God's good. Her family, security and innocence had been stolen away. Without the proof she craved, her profound losses would never make sense. She would never be complete.

Daniel eased from the edge of his chair to press his knees to the floor beside Erin. He offered his open hand as he would to a frightened animal. A sign of comfort, lacking all aggression. After a moment of hesitation, she slipped her left palm into his and laced their fingers together as her gaze implored his face.

"Erin, God's ways are not our ways. He sees with eternal eyes and the vision He has for us in this world is beyond anything our minds can conceive. This side of heaven, most believers will never understand the purpose for what seems like life's random events. But Jeremiah 29:11 assures us God has a plan to give us a future and a hope. When we have no proof, we exercise faith."

As if his words had siphoned off her energy, Erin leaned to the left allowing her head to rest against his shoulder.

"Sweet lady," he whispered as he slipped his arm behind her in support. "Every treasure you have stored in this binder is confirmation that you were exactly where God wanted you to be."

"Even though my rightful place was with you and Dana?"

She asked the question Daniel had been trying to come to terms with for years. Maybe if Erin could accept the answer, he could, too.

"Well, you see, that's where God really does some of His best work. When our free will conflicts with a pretty simple plan and turns it into a confusing mess, He can still use it for His glory if we get back in line with His Word and cooperate. And your willingness to go where He sends you has produced some pictures in situations where words could never, ever do justice. Journalists wrote about that tsunami in Indonesia all day long, but it was your photos that moved thousands of people toward relief efforts."

The outside corners of her eyes radiated tiny lines as she concentrated, processing his words.

"You've followed my career," she said softly, as if shocked.

"How could you expect anything else of me? Your talent confirmed my belief in Dana's future. She'll be a winner at whatever she wants to pursue, just like her beautiful mama." Daniel assured the woman whose head still rested on his shoulder.

She exhaled a breath, as if releasing uncertainty from deep inside. The eyes that had been so anxious only moments before softly fluttered to a close. Where muscles in her face had been tense, they now relaxed. As Daniel cradled her tenderly, he realized that for the first time since she'd arrived in his home, here with her cheek warm against his shoulder, Erin seemed at peace.

Was there a chance she might stop fighting the *cozy* feeling of family?

Specifically Daniel's family?

Her breathing slowed, deepened. He shifted away.

"Um, as much as I hate to disturb you, I wouldn't want Mama or Dana to see us like this."

Erin's eyes flew wide as she noticed the doors leading to the common hallway of the house were open.

"Good point," she agreed as they moved apart and Daniel resumed his place on a nearby chair. "We wouldn't want them to get the wrong idea."

"Definitely not." The tenderness in Daniel's voice was gone, replaced by the no-nonsense tone of a responsible father.

Definitely not? Had the heart-to-heart moment been one-sided? Even with zero experience, Erin felt certain she was interpreting Daniel's caring behavior correctly. Had she been wrong? Was exposing her vulnerability a mistake?

He stood and prepared to leave. "Can I tempt you with milk and cookies before we call it a night?"

"A snack sounds perfect," she agreed, going along with his change of subject.

"I'll be right back."

As soon as he was across the threshold, she threw her legs over the side of the chaise, tipped forward from the waist and used the momentum of her shoulders to pull to her feet. Using her left hand to press her right forearm close to her body, she shuffled across the floor to the bottom of the bed. She depressed the foot pedal to lower the level of the mattress. Once she was seated with her legs stretched out before her, she pulled the covers up to her waist and worked the buttons of the television remote rather deftly in spite of her sluggish right hand.

"On a scale of one to ten, I'd give that an eight." Daniel spoke from the doorway, having completed his kitchen mission sooner than she'd expected.

"You snuck up on me," she tried to sound offended. "Nobody is supposed to see that until I have it down to a perfect ten."

He set the tray with two glasses of milk and a plate of fresh oatmeal cookies on her bedside table.

"Well, you don't have much further to go. And I gotta tell you, it's a relief to see firsthand that I don't need to worry about taking you with us to the Double-S."

Her stomach lurched at his words. The sweet aroma of the cookies no longer appealed.

"Does that mean you think I'll be okay here by myself?"

"Goodness no," he dismissed her comment. Pffffed at the very idea. "With that performance, you just eliminated all my concerns about the long trip and the accommodations at the main house. After another week with your PT, you'll be in shape to ride and rope."

He selected the plumpest cookie, dunked it into his glass of milk and then popped it into his waiting mouth.

"We'll be hitching up the wagon train and headin' west at sunrise one week from today. All you have to decide is whether you want to ride five hundred miles listening to Mama's singin' or Dana's snorin'."

Chapter Nine

As they drove beneath the archway that announced their arrival at the ranch a week later, the Stabler family history Erin acquired during the long road trip began to come to life.

"Stabler and Sons" was shortened to "Double-S" after the death of Daniel's father when the boys were still in high school. LaVerne had insisted they mark the occasion by rededicating and renaming her sons' inheritance. Each year on their last night together, the family honored their patriarch with country songs and cowboy prayers beneath a sunset summer sky.

The overlapping "SS" fashioned of thick black wrought iron was suspended high above the entry to the property between two tall knotted pines, stripped bare by an axe and smoothed artfully by the West Texas wind. Erin lowered her window and poked her head out catching the spicy smell of mesquite.

"Daniel, I didn't expect the sheer immenseness of this place." As far as she could see in every direction, the land was enclosed and marked with their curlicue brand on hundreds of fence posts.

"The maintenance of all this barbed wire must be a full-time job for somebody."

"Well, we have seasonal workers who stay in the bunkhouse when it's not rented out to hunters. And the Torres family lives on the property and helps with year-round operations. We built them a nice cabin on the western ridge." He pointed in the direction the sun was headed.

"So, you have caretakers?"

"I guess that's the truth of it, but they're more like family to us. Isadore and Elena were migrant workers until their third son was born and Mama convinced them to stay on full time and become citizens."

"Bet that was an easy sell."

"Yeah, considering the poverty they left across the border. But remember, we're talking about LaVerne, here. Why do you think me and Jake built the cabin so far from the main house?" Erin enjoyed the charming smile and half wink that began to punctuate his tongue-in-cheek comments.

There had been no further private moments between the two of them, but Daniel continued to show special kindness when Dana and Erin included him in their time together.

His hand lightly steadied the small of Erin's back during their evening walks around the cul-de-sac. He was available and courteous for even her smallest need. If conditions were different, Erin might interpret Daniel's actions to be what was once called old-fashioned courting. But she knew better.

"Is that your family home?" She pointed to a cluster of

gabled rooflines, hazy in the afternoon heat. Jagged mountains far in the distance made a breathtaking backdrop.

"Actually, those are the stables and the corral is just beyond them. The bunkhouse and Mama's place are up the road, you'll see them in a minute."

"And your brother's family?"

"Jake built Becky a stucco hacienda over that first hill so they're close by if Mama needs anything. But my sister-in-law was smart to put some distance between herself and LaVerne. She can't sneak up without a cloud of dust announcing her arrival."

With the big Cadillac right behind them, Daniel kept a slow and considerate pace to hold down the gravel kicked up by his truck tires. Erin was fascinated by the interesting sights he pointed out during the half mile drive from the highway to the working compound.

He pulled over to offer her a good look at the network of classic red barns and what he referred to as livestock pens. LaVerne gave two short blasts of her horn and passed the SUV. Dana waved them eagerly onward, a wide smile on her face.

"She seems pretty happy to be here," Erin noted.

"I suspect that's true on some level, but it's more likely just relief that the boring ride is over."

"A person has to be awake to be bored. Dana was dead to the world in your mama's backseat the entire way." Erin was incredulous at the girl's capacity for sleep. "I don't think she woke up more than once and that was at the truck stop where we bought corn dogs."

"That's been her road-trip system for years and it works for me. She stays up all night packing, watching TV and loading music on her iPod. When I give her the ten-minute warning, she drags her pillow and blanket out to the truck, puts on her earphones and burrows into her den to hibernate. That way I don't have to listen to her racket and she doesn't have to be subjected to mine."

Erin admired the solidly built and well-maintained buildings while she considered this latest explanation of the give and take between Daniel and Dana. It was a marvel how parent and child had cooperated for years to find agreeable solutions whether it was intentional or otherwise. Erin couldn't recall a single time in her youth when she'd been permitted the freedom to work out issues on her own terms. It was a liberty Dana took for granted.

Father, I'm so grateful that this child won't ever experience the harshness that dominated my life at her age.

Dana was sixteen. At sixteen Erin had been completely under somebody's control. It wasn't until she'd been released from foster care, on the verge of adulthood that she could decide anything for herself. And by then, not only was there nobody to argue, there wasn't anybody to even care.

Until Daniel.

Erin returned her attention to the present, to the handsome man beside her who'd been talking while her mind had been wandering.

"I mean, how can any adult honestly say they enjoy rap? Even the Christian variety makes my head pound."

"Then why do you listen to it?" she asked.

"I just told you, it's our arrangement. When we're driving around town, Dana keeps the headphones off so we can talk and we take turns controlling the radio."

"Can't you just overrule the music she chooses if you don't like it?"

He cocked his head to the right and sighted down his nose at Erin, every inch a detective. "You didn't hear a word I said, did you?"

"You were talking about taking turns," she said, hoping the light defensiveness in her voice would cover her short wander through the minefields of her memory.

"Okay, so maybe you were sorta payin' attention." He gave her a small break. "But to answer your question, no, I don't overrule her music. How else will I know what the kids are listening to? I just grit my teeth and hold my tongue if the lyrics bother me. Then I wait for another time and casually coach her about dicey subjects I pick up in the music."

As Erin considered his strategy, her respect for his parenting notched even higher. She prayed her influence in Dana's life would never erode the strong foundation Daniel had laid.

"In case nobody's told you lately, you're an incredible father. You always have Dana's best interest at heart and keeping the peace in your relationship seems to be something you pursue one hundred percent of the time."

He put the SUV in gear and eased it back onto the road.

"Thanks, but I don't deserve such high praise. The truth is I only try ninety-nine percent of the time and I enjoy that last wayward percent far too much." His tone matched the grin that curled his lips. "You see, when it's my turn to control the radio, I make her listen to the Grand Ole Opry."

It was always comforting for Daniel to be home again. Sort of.

He was never sure what kind of greeting he'd get from Jake. This time of year he would be knee-deep in details, glad to see his brother show up but mostly so he could shuck the responsibility of the ranch and give his full attention to the barbecue. It was just as well since Daniel preferred the company of Isadore and his boys to the brother whose needling was the proverbial thorn in Daniel's side. He figured Jake's passive-aggressive way with a wisecrack was God's reminder that there was a more worrisome reason than the western cottonmouth to pursue a career in the city.

As Daniel stepped down and rounded the back of his Expedition, a dinged-up, red Ford pickup ground to a stop nearby. Jake hopped out.

"Well, look who decided to grace us with his presence," he drawled. "I hope this little side trip on your way to the Texas Ranger Hall of Fame won't slow you down, little brother."

In spite of the cutting words, Jake reached to shake Daniel's hand and then pulled him close for a bear hug.

"It's g-good to see you, t-too," Daniel stuttered during the back-thumping welcome Jake was administering.

"Was that your mystery woman ridin' shotgun with Mama?"

Daniel shook his head. "Dana's always a mystery to me, but I don't think she's who you meant."

"Your Dana rode all the way from Houston with LaVerne?" With a leather-gloved fist Jake tipped the brim of his workaday hat back on his head. "How much did that bribe set you back?"

"Not a dime. I think those two are finally in cahoots." Daniel rolled his eyes at the thought of his mother's and daughter's subtle matchmaking. But Erin had made her intentions clear from the beginning, so they were wasting their time. Still, in the evenings when they were all sipping sweet tea on the back patio, Daniel couldn't help wondering how things might have been different.

"So, where is the family celebrity?" Jake demanded.

Daniel pulled the handle opening the passenger door, then stepped aside. "Erin, as much as it pains me to admit it, this is my brother. Jake, this is Erin Gray."

Jake whipped his head in a double take. "It's nice to finally meet you." He accepted her left hand, squinting hard at her face.

"Are you sure?" She laughed. "The way you're staring makes me think I wasn't what you expected."

"Sorry, ma'am. I never had much of a poker face. Truth is I thought you'd look at least a little bit like Dana. She sure doesn't favor our family, so who does she take after?"

Daniel waited for Erin's response. As much as he'd wondered the same thing, he knew better than to question Erin. Even Dana had tap-danced around the subject, but never asked outright.

"That answer is probably buried so deep in the roots of the family tree that we'll never know for sure," Erin said, her answer vague as always, steering conversation away from her past.

"Well, whoever she resembles, it's still a sight better than looking like her old man." Jake laughed at his own comment.

"That's a fact," Daniel agreed. "I tell her all the time there are worse things than skin that won't tan. She could have my knobby knees and scrawny backside. Daddy always said it looked like a tribe of Navajos moved out of the seat of my jeans."

Jake clapped a hand on Daniel's shoulder. "Dana should thank the good Lord every night for her curves. I know my girls would love some."

The two men unloaded the SUV in the companionable way their father had taught them to work. Each trip home was a reminder of their ability to partner without words, using silent head jerks and one-syllable grunts to communicate. It was always best to keep Jake too busy for conversation.

"Thanks for the help," Daniel said after the last bag was set on the wraparound veranda. "See you for supper?"

"Yep, we'll all be back by six. Becky has a brisket in the oven and our girls are anxious to see Dana's latest gadgets."

"Welcome to the Double-S, Erin." Jake nodded and touched the brim of his hat before climbing back into his truck.

She'd made herself comfortable on the front porch glider in need of its annual coat of candy apple red. Daniel's heart thumped hard realizing Erin had to be the prettiest thing ever to dangle bare feet from that creaky old chair.

"You should always keep shoes on when you're outside," he warned, knowing firsthand about scorpion stings and fire ant bites. "And not rubber flip-flops either, proper boots that will protect you from bugs and snakes."

She pulled her knees up, pressing her heels to the edge of the glider. "I know better, I just couldn't resist shucking my socks and feeling this dry air on my toes." She reached for her things to begin the cumbersome process of putting on stockings and shoes with one hand.

"Here, let me help," he offered. Before she could object and he could think better of it, Daniel scooped Erin into his arms and carried her across the threshold. It was a pretend moment, but he was finally bringing his bride home. How many times had he regretted not taking Erin to meet his family? But she'd flatly refused, insisting the moment was never right. And it probably still wasn't right, but God had given Daniel this opportunity and he'd make the best of it for as long as it lasted. What was the harm in showing Erin what could have been?

He carried Erin into the huge kitchen that was the epicenter of the spacious main floor and deposited her on a tall stool at the counter.

"What's wrong?" Dana and LaVerne's alarmed voices chorused. His mama hurried across the pine plank floor. "Don't tell me something already got ahold of you."

"I'm fine." Erin waved away any concern. "Daniel just gave me VIP taxi service from the porch."

"Dana, will you help your grandma canvas the ranch for a pair of boots that will fit Erin, please? I should have thought about this before we left Houston." He'd have enjoyed visiting his favorite Western wear store to custom fit her with a stylish pair of ropers. Even the simplest act of kindness pleased her so. She'd be fun to spoil.

"Daniel, it's no big deal. I'll be fine with sneakers."

"We'll see that you get whatever you need," LaVerne assured everyone.

"The only thing I need is time to take this place in." Erin's voice held a faraway quality as she tipped her head back to view the twenty-foot vaulted ceiling.

Daniel remembered being a small boy, watching as a crane hoisted the heavy cross beams into place. How happy his parents had been when the four of them had moved from what was now the bunkhouse into this cavernous home.

"LaVerne, I could just sit in this kitchen or on your front porch and never want to leave."

A snort of laughter burst from Dana.

"That's what everybody says when they first get here. Just give Grandma Verne and Uncle Jake a couple of days to figure out where you fit into the labor program. You'll be plotting your escape along with the rest of us."

"I beg your pardon, Sleeping Beauty." Her grandmother stood with arms akimbo, all business in a blue checked apron. "Helping with the chores never hurt anybody. And if you keep running that mouth, I'll find some toilets that need scrubbing right after you finish rummaging in the tack room and the storage barn for a spare pair of boots for your mama." LaVerne motioned toward the back door with her thumb.

Dana's eyes sought Erin's, no doubt looking for an ally.

"An eight would be perfect, but I can live with a half size on either side if that's the best you can do."

LaVerne turned back to the business of pantry inventory and Daniel bit his lip to keep from laughing at Dana as the screen door bounced on its hinges behind her.

"Well done." Daniel applauded. "You handled that like a pro."

"I've been watching some great role models the past couple of weeks." Erin nodded toward Daniel and his mama.

"Well, thank you, but we've both been operating in 'company mode.'" He lowered his voice and leaned in close. "You're about to see LaVerne large and in charge of her own territory. Just do as she tells you and no-body'll get hurt."

"I wouldn't consider doing otherwise."

"Then you'll be the only woman on this place who feels that way. Becky's every bit as bull-headed as Mama and her four girls would just as soon eat dirt as admit their grandma knows best. But you'll see. After a few hundred folks show up next week, LaVerne's ingenuity will save the day when something unexpected crops up."

"With so many people coming and going, I just hope I won't be in the way."

He rolled his eyes at the thought of this quiet lady being an imposition. Now that they were home, he was truly glad she'd come.

"I'll put your things in my old room." He pointed toward a hallway off the kitchen. "The master is two doors down so Mama's nearby if you need anything. I'll keep Dana company in the crow's nest." He pointed to the steps that led to the second floor.

"Are you sure you don't mind giving me your room?"

"Actually, Dana and I prefer a buffer between us and Mama. Anytime you're ready to practice your climbing skills, we'll make room for you upstairs."

LaVerne backed out of the pantry clutching her grocery list and overheard his last few words.

"Son, don't be inhospitable. Of course Erin's not climbing those steps. Put her things in your room so I can keep an eye on her."

"That's a great idea, Mama. I should have thought of it myself."

He gave Erin a conspiratorial wink when what he really wanted to give her was a welcome to West Texas kiss.

Chapter Ten

Suppertime was a cross between a rodeo and a picnic.

Erin counted a dozen pair of weather-worn cowboy boots lined up in a mud rack just inside the front door of the expansive family home. Most of the stocking-footed guests were decked out in Western wear and all of them had brought covered platters or casserole dishes to contribute to the evening meal.

The Torres family arrived first. The *boys* Daniel had mentioned were much older than expected. All college-educated, the three had come back to work the Double-S after graduation. The naturalized Americans truly were the Stablers' extended family.

Jake's wife and four girls poured through the door, next. They grabbed Dana and swept her out to the bunk-house away from the adults. Erin connected with Becky from their first hug. Even if it was just a wives' tale that men married women like their mamas, it certainly applied to Daniel's brother. He'd found a no-nonsense lady who could give as good as she got from LaVerne, deal with migrant workers in their native language and still wrangle a houseful of kids known for bringing piglets and baby skunks inside for a visit.

Supper was a mouthwatering assortment of roasted meats, fresh vegetables and home-baked breads. Afterward Erin sipped iced tea and visited with the other women as they washed, dried and put away the many place settings of Fiesta pottery.

"LaVerne, after raising boys, was it hard for you to adjust to all these granddaughters?" Erin asked.

"I still haven't adjusted," she grumbled. "Jake's girls would rather inoculate calves than learn to bake biscuits. And since operating the microwave is about as technical as I get, Dana and I don't have much common ground, which I'm sure you've already noticed."

LaVerne turned an affectionate gaze to the dark-eyed Mexican woman at her side. "I'm just glad I spoke enough Spanish to be close to Elena's boys as they were comin' up. Why, Miguel is like one of my own."

"*Si,* and we considered giving our oldest to you legally during his last year of high school." Elena turned to Erin. "That boy only survives today by the grace of Senora Stabler. When Isadore was ready to lock Miguel in a horse trailer and throw away the key, *la* Senora intervened."

LaVerne swatted away the accolade with her damp dish towel. "I merely pointed out to Miguel how fortunate he was to have a father when my sons were without one at his age."

"*Honestamente?*" There was disbelief in Elena's voice. "All you did was encourage my Miguel to appreciate his papa?"

"Well, that and twenty dollars for each passing grade on his report card." LaVerne rubbed her thumb and forefinger together indicating money had changed hands. "It got the desired results."

"*Yo lo supe!* I knew it," Elena cried. "That boy always had more money than the other two. No wonder he could afford a car for graduation."

"Cash didn't work with Oscar and Alano. They responded better to boots and riding tack." LaVerne held her palms outward in defense. "Besides, it's a little late to hold spoiling your kids against me, now."

"You may call it 'spoiling' if you like, but I call it 'bribery.' Either way, it worked and we are grateful to you for it, *mi* amigo."

Erin knew of the carrot-and-stick approach, but in foster care there was mostly evidence of the stick end of the philosophy. Staying clear of punishment was the only reward.

"LaVerne, it sounds like you just need to figure out what appeals to the girls," Erin suggested.

"That's just it. Grandma Stabler only bothers to spoon out sugar to the men folk," Becky announced.

"Meaning?" The way LaVerne fixed her gray eyes on the serving bowl in her hands while she waited on Becky's answer told Erin this was a touchy, old subject.

"Meaning that the only approach you take with your granddaughters is to boss them around. There's never a choice for them to make. It's Grandma Verne's way or the highway so they simply stay away."

"Well, Becky Stabler, if that ain't the pot calling the kettle black."

Becky loaded a stack of colorful dishes into the glass-fronted cabinets then looked to Erin to explain.

"I'm their mother. They're supposed to hate me. But she's their only grandma and that's a relationship they should enjoy. LaVerne could have our girls eating out of her hand, but she'd rather have them toeing the line every minute of the day."

"Those girls don't need coddling," LaVerne insisted. "They need to be strong, independent. Women have to earn their own way and make smart decisions instead of marrying for security. Erin, you have a modern woman's work ethic. What do you say?"

Erin knew a little something about cross fire. And though this was friendly fire, she was still caught in it.

She squeezed the glob of putty that was her constant companion and considered her response carefully. On the one hand, LaVerne's point was valid. Erin had observed just enough of her own mother to know the path she'd taken was not worth repeating. But on the other hand, modeling responsibility would never trump unconditional love. Just as Erin had missed so many experiences with Dana, LaVerne was losing opportunities with her granddaughters that might never come along again.

But this was neither the time nor the place to share that insight.

"Ladies, considering my track record, I feel completely unqualified to offer an opinion."

"What a cop-out," Becky teased.

"That's hogwash," LaVerne agreed with her daughter-in-law and the two fell back into comfortable work.

With the clean-up complete, Becky called to the men who were involved in a noisy baseball debate.

"Gentlemen, if y'all can forget about the pennant race for a few minutes and come back to the kitchen, there's fresh gingerbread and hot coffee over here for you."

Everyone agreeably padded toward the large plank-style table, chairs scraping as they pulled close to enjoy being together for the fragrant dessert.

Becky drew a thick folder from her quilted tote and handed it to Jake who kissed her on the cheek, gratitude in his eyes. A pang of envy pierced Erin's heart as she watched the two.

"Thanks for remembering this, hon. Now we can nail down some assignments and get a jump on things in the morning."

As Dana had predicted, Daniel's brother had jobs for everybody. Even the five girls who'd opted for dinner and video games in the bunkhouse had assignment sheets of their own. Until the trophies were awarded and the last aluminum can had been hauled to the recycling center, everybody would be busy.

Everybody but Erin. She was feeling about as useless as poison ivy when LaVerne plunked down a box designed to hold a pair of Tony Lama's.

"You found me some cowboy boots, already?"

"Sure did," Becky announced. "But they're back at our place. I'll run them over to you first thing tomorrow."

"Then what's in here?"

"I'm so glad you asked." LaVerne smirked and removed the lid to reveal hundreds of snapshots stacked tightly inside. "There's another dozen boxes just like this in my closet."

Erin glanced at Daniel. His elbows rested on the tabletop beside her. He grinned as he forked up his last bite of gingerbread. "Did you think she was kiddin' when she said she was gonna put you to work?"

Her knee tingled pleasantly where he bumped his against hers. Erin gulped black coffee, imagining herself stuck inside the house sorting pictures while everybody else enjoyed the incredible scenery outdoors. She wanted to watch Daniel and Dana handle the day-to-day needs of the ranch. To catch a close-up look at the baby animals the girls talked about. To get to know everybody she'd met today. As well-traveled as she was, Erin had never been on a ranch or to a cook-off of any kind and was looking forward to the experiences. The very thought of spending her days cooped up sorting hundreds of somebody else's pictures made her heart sink. But it was the least she could do to help after these folks had welcomed her into their lives.

"So, my job will be to organize all these photos?"

"Of course not," LaVerne dismissed the idea. She tugged the lid back on the box and moved it to the counter.

"I'm saving that for my senior years. Besides, today you couldn't tell a Southern Yankee smoker from a John Deere tractor. But you'll know the difference in no time, if you get out there in the middle of things. Just watch and photograph all the preparations and rub elbows with the contestants." LaVerne snapped her fingers at a new thought. "Why, with you winnin' that Pulitzer Surprise thing, we might even be able to talk folks into paying to get their picture made."

Erin felt Daniel tense beside her, he sat up taller.

"Now hold on a minute, Mama. Asking Erin to snap a bunch of random shots is one thing. Making money off her reputation is altogether another. We never agreed that would be part of the plan."

Plan? There was a plan, and Daniel cared enough to be in on it?

Erin felt the pleasant warmth of his nearness settle

around her spirit as if he'd hugged her close. Unseen by the others, she pressed her palm over his knee beneath the table. The way his pupils dilated confirmed that his attention was all hers.

"It's okay, Daniel. In fact, it's a great idea." Erin's gaze fixed on his and she nodded in agreement with LaVerne. "I'm not a portrait artist, but if people are willing to spend a few extra dollars for a good cause, count me in."

"Let's talk about it privately," he closed the subject.

"So you're willin' to use that fancy camera and rumble with the locals?" LaVerne bulldozed ahead.

The flicker of an idea ignited Erin's mental pilot light. It had been years since she'd accepted an assignment that had more local color than global impact. Where she might once have dismissed this as fund-raising fluff, today she recognized the importance of a small community's generosity. She smiled at the wistful notion of human beings enjoying life instead of struggling to survive its hardships.

"Photographs of happy people are not exactly what I'm known for but I'm willing to give it a try. Besides, it's the least I can do to repay everyone's kindness."

"We're not being kind, Erin. We're being family."

All heads turned toward Daniel's brother.

"You're our Dana's mama and that makes you one of us. We wouldn't have it any other way."

Erin murmured her thanks to Jake who gave the same half wink she'd begun to treasure from Daniel.

She lowered her eyes to hide the sting of recognition. Was the charming blink only a coy family mannerism? And was Jake in on *the plan,* too?

* * *

Daniel stood on the front porch and watched Jake's taillights shrink to the size of the fireflies that hovered over the small patch of lawn. He thought they'd never leave. For the past two hours, he'd been torn between his desire to quite literally kiss Erin for her cooperation and his urge to give LaVerne "what for" by dropping a carton of eggs on her clean kitchen floor. His mama had no business setting Erin up like that and he intended to let her know how he felt about it.

But first Daniel had to examine how he felt about Erin.

The qualities that had drawn him to her in their youth were slowly resurfacing in her reserved mannerisms, her quiet conversations, her willingness to work hard and her determination to be independent. Though she continued to be modest about her career, the unmistakable pride of accomplishment glimmered in her eyes.

Erin's fear that had once seemed a constant presence was now an occasional shadow. But Daniel suspected the change was more a product of mind over memory than it was the defeat of demons. Erin would have to face them down at some point, just as he would have to admit to decisions that haunted him.

How many days did he have left? Should he stick with his plan? His heart thudded as he considered what failure could mean.

Though all was well at the moment, a distant fire bell seemed to clang in the back of Daniel's mind. Erin was improving every day. So, time was running out. His intention to have her experience a loving family was a game of chance with long odds, high stakes and few possible outcomes. Any time now, Erin would realize she was fit to go back to her job and she'd leave. Or she'd figure out the Stablers were an over-the-top, crazy clan and she'd still leave. Or she'd come to understand that being part of an over-the-top, crazy clan wasn't so bad. And after her efforts to bond with Dana, if Erin went back to her life anyway, he had no doubt Dana would fight to go, too.

The final possibility was one Daniel refused to consider. Dana was his only child and she wasn't going anywhere. Not even with Erin.

He glanced toward the screen door. It was the end of a long day. Maybe Erin was too tired to join him on the porch glider after all. He settled on the creaky old thing aware it was a snug fit for two adults. He tipped his head back and stared into the vastness. An endless canopy of stars spread overhead like the Lord had rolled it out to welcome Daniel home.

"Father, thank You for Your glorious handiwork. I see Your fingerprints in this black Texas sky. Is this what Erin feels in an African jungle or an Indonesian rain forest? Could this ache in my chest be what she experiences when she comes close to catching that miracle? Lord, I'm trying to understand Erin so I can think beyond my own needs. I'm trying to consider what makes her heart sing so I can accept those restless parts of her. Grant me the serenity to accept the things I cannot change, courage to change the things I can and the wisdom to know the difference."

His father had taught the principles of the Serenity Prayer long before Daniel knew it had a title. Soon he would have to rely on that acceptance, courage and wisdom to get him through the day when Erin would choose between two lives a world apart.

"Am I too late?" Erin's question was barely louder than the lonely whisper of the constant wind.

"Not at all."

As she took the seat beside him, Daniel scooted closer to the arm of the glider to make room. Even so, the length of their bodies touched; shoulders pressed, hips crowded, thigh against thigh, knee to knee. Daniel swept his arm high and then settled it along the cool metal resting his hand on the chair's rusty corner.

They sat in silence. Their lack of words was natural, as if they did it every day.

"I apologize for what happened in there." He was the first to speak. "Mama shouldn't have put you on the spot like that."

"I take it her suggestion wasn't an original part of *the plan?*"

He sighed, shook his head. He knew Erin had caught that comment even if she'd let it pass.

"Erin, it's nothing more than me and Mama agreeing to engage you in physical activity whenever we can. We don't want you to feel like you did the wrong thing by comin' with us instead of stayin' in Houston with Christina the Hun. If you keep up with your free-weight exercises and rest your back regularly, we figured being outside, moving around and using your arms a lot would make up for not having daily PT. I even got clearance from your orthopedic doctor to get you on horseback for a gentle ride if you're willing. He said it would be good for backside muscles as long as you take it easy."

Erin leaned away and tilted her head to the right so she could look up into his face.

"How am I ever going to show you my gratitude?"

"Not necessary." He shook his head.

"That's where we continually disagree." The faraway crescent moon cast a glow that illuminated her glistening eyes. "Daniel, I do not deserve to be in this amazing place with you and Dana, being treated as if I belong here. Feelings that I can't even name are rushing up from deep inside my soul. It's overwhelming." She paused as if hesitant over what she'd say next. "And if I could wrap both arms around you and let half of this emotion overflow into your spirit so you could share this experience, I would."

As his pulse quickened, Daniel let his arm drop from the back of the chair to drape behind Erin. His fingers curled to cup the shoulder he squeezed softly. As she had that night in his home, Erin sighed and leaned her body against his, turning so her cheek lay near his heart. He folded her close, his arms and emotions melting around her.

He was certain she could feel the thumping beneath his cotton shirt where her hand rested on his chest. He pressed his lips to her forehead, a kiss barely grazing her skin. They clung for endless seconds as the cadence of their breathing became one.

"Nice," she whispered.

"Very." His response was husky with the urge to tip her face upward, to capture her mouth against his.

The warm wind brushed them as a lone coyote howled in the distance. With his pulse a silent hammering in his ears, Daniel remembered their surroundings. He blinked away the pleasant thought of a kiss and straightened a bit in the glider.

"If that was more than the hug you had in mind,

you'll have to pardon me." He also hoped his words covered the schoolboy jitters he felt.

Where her body still pressed to his, a shudder passed between them. She seemed to be struggling with a flood of words that needed release.

"Daniel, I'm the one who needs the pardon. You're the kindest man I've ever known. What is it that makes you able to forgive?" Her voice quivered with the question.

"Shh." He touched a fingertip to her lips. "I don't deserve the credit you're givin' me. Despite all my prayers and best intentions, I've never been able to let go of all the anger from our past."

He feared there would always be bitter and empty places in his heart. And at this moment with Erin in his arms again, Daniel accepted what he'd always known. Only God can soothe and fill those places and it was time to let Erin off the hook.

"I understand." Erin gave him absolution, then pressed trembling lips tight as a fat tear threatened to spill from the corner of one eye. After gulping a deep breath she continued. "Please allow me to say this, Daniel. Thank you for raising my beautiful daughter. Thank you for being a man of your word. Thank you for protecting me when you must have exposed your own heart a thousand times to do it. And thank you for coming to my rescue when there was nobody else." She gave up the effort to hold back her feelings and let them flow.

Chapter Eleven

Daniel felt warmth pool in his eyes. He'd cried buckets of tears over the estrangement of their little family and the pain could still break the surface at the drop of a hat. His arms closed around her, pulling her carefully into the circle of his embrace while she wept for a heartache she believed no one could understand. Sins no one could forgive.

Secrets burned in both their chests. He agonized over truths that could solidify their future or tear it apart forever. Confession would be good for his soul, but Daniel held the words in check, praying for mercy on the day when there would be no more hiding from decisions of the past.

Erin's quiet weeping turned to embarrassed sniffles and heavy sighs as she regained composure.

"Don't even think about making another apology," Daniel warned as he swiped moisture from his lashes. "Letting some of the pressure leak out with tears is relief I've learned to understand all too well. Every night since that human-trafficking scam was turned over to my team I've felt like crying. The details would break anybody with a heart. Most of the dead were no older than Isadore and Elena's boys. What some people will do for money is unconscionable."

"Man's inhumanity to man is incredible, isn't it?" she murmured.

Oftentimes Daniel wished for the ability to close his mind against the images stored there. He couldn't imagine what Erin must have witnessed in her work. "I s'pose you've seen more injustice and cruelty than anyone ever should. How have you kept it from making you crazy?"

She shifted in the chair but stayed in the crook of his arm.

"I don't dwell on it," was her simple answer.

"But your pictures bring it back to you over and over again. How can you not be affected?"

She drew in and blew out several deep breaths.

"On the battlefield, a photographer has to keep an emotional distance, just like you do during an investigation. I guess the difference is that I see so much of life through a tiny lens that it keeps me from connecting with what's happening right in front of me. When I look at my work later, I realize I probably should have been running for my life instead of concentrating on the shot. But in that split second, the image is my only concern."

"Still, it's hard to even look on death, much less take pictures of it."

"But it's the right thing to do for people who can't speak for themselves. Sometimes a picture is the only way to tell a story the world doesn't want to hear."

Daniel considered the incredible strength and wisdom of the woman pressed so near to his heart.

"Now it's my turn to compliment you, Erin. You are the bravest lady I've ever known." Worried his praise would make her choke up again, he hurried on. "But please don't ever tell LaVerne I said so, 'cause she thinks that title belongs to her."

The tense moment dissolved along with their brief burst of laughter. He returned to a lighter subject.

"So you honestly don't mind being our Double-S roving reporter? It's a bit of an insult to your credentials."

"As you said, life can be cruel and unjust. I'm quite content to spend a few days training my camera on smiling people for a change. I'll go back to the trenches soon enough."

I'll go back to the trenches soon enough.

With her simple statement, Daniel's full heart began to deflate. No matter how welcoming or enjoyable she found her circumstances, they were never meant to be forever. Not to Erin, anyway. Somewhere on the road between Houston and Fort Stockton, he'd stopped seeing things objectively and started pretending otherwise. He was a fool to somehow think what was growing between Erin and Dana could include him.

The high-pitched laughter of young ladies resounded in the distance like wind chimes stirred to life. Movement sensors triggered security lights that sprung to attention illuminating Dana and her four cousins. They shuffled along the pathway from the bunkhouse lowering their voices to share some private humor. Daniel stretched his arm away from Erin and pushed to his feet before Dana was close enough to see them together.

Yes, he had to stop imagining things. But more importantly, he had to make sure his daughter understood that very soon they would return to life as they'd always known it. Without the woman who was making them whole.

"Where are you young ladies headed? I thought you'd be sacked out by now." It felt good to tease the girls. He knew full well their summer routine centered on staying up late and steering clear of LaVerne.

"Hey, Uncle Daniel," they called. The four Becky lookalikes climbed the steps and hugged him in turn. Each skinny girl was as different from his curvy daughter as the Big Bend was from the Big Apple. They were West Texas country; handy with a rifle, a cattle prod and adjusting the hitch on a horse trailer. Dana was all about Wi-Fi, iPhones and IMs. Contrast her purple spikes and dozen silver rings with their sun-bleached ponytails and freckled noses and it was pretty clear that in these parts his girl was a duck out of water. When the rest of the Stabler clan began to arrive, Dana's current confidence might evaporate like steam from a teakettle. He planned to give her self-image a boost via horse and lasso in the next few days.

"We're gonna see if there's any gingerbread and ice cream left." At seventeen, Tina Sue was the oldest and bossiest of the bunch. "But we don't wanna disturb Grandma Verne. Do you know if she's gone to bed yet?"

"The coast is clear," he assured them. "Just keep your voices down and don't forget to rinse your dishes when you're finished."

Dana brought up the rear as the line of girls crept toward the door, muffling their approach by keeping the heels of their boots from touching the wooden planks. Daniel grinned, remembering the same effort he and Jake had made on countless occasions. His mama was probably sitting in her bedroom right now, smiling along with him just as she had back then.

"Butter bean," he called before she took her turn through the screen door. "Everybody has an early start in the morning so don't stay up too late."

"Yes, sir," she dutifully replied. "And Daddy?"

"What is it, baby girl?"

"You can sit back down with Erin now. We won't be outside again for at least thirty minutes."

The closing door muffled the pleasant sound of her laughter.

Erin knew firsthand that what was said about the marines was true; they accomplished more by 9:00 a.m. than most folks did all day. But during her first week on the Double-S, she discovered the same condition exists for ranching families. Especially those motivated to raise funds for a Christian boys' home.

Daniel and Dana were on horseback fifteen minutes after daybreak and Erin had a hundred digital images to prove it. Seeing the two of them sit tall in the saddle was another emotional moment that took her by surprise. She'd been on the brink of tears or laughter since the day she'd been installed on the sun porch in Houston. Things had only intensified since their arrival in Fort Stockton.

In the quiet of Daniel's boyhood room, God revealed a surprising truth to Erin; the same sense of belonging she'd begun to feel in Houston had followed her out west. The blackness of the night that had always been her hiding place was now a silent time to listen for the snoring of LaVerne, identify the stirring of Dana, take comfort in the solid presence of Daniel. Where could she go in the world and replicate this peace? What had never even been a concern was now Erin's growing worry.

She would miss them terribly when she left.

"Will you ride with us today?" Dana called.

Erin was seated comfortably in a thick futon chair just inside the livestock barn. Jake had hauled the bulky seat down from the bunkhouse so she'd have a breezy spot to put her feet up on the five-gallon bucket that served as her ottoman. He was as thoughtful of others as he was critical of his only sibling. Any minute now Erin expected Daniel to tell his brother to shove it. But Daniel shrugged off Jake's jibes like a horse's tail swiped away an ornery fly. Everyone else seemed to go along, as if the insults were funny or somehow deserved.

Erin bit her tongue till it was bloody. Years of exposure to hard-shelled marines had taught her to speak her mind if what she had to say could make a positive impact. Something had to give, and soon.

Dana reined an aging paint mare to the edge of the corral. "Did you hear me, Erin?"

"I did, I was thinking about my answer. I'm not sure I'm ready."

"Don't be afraid. I'll even let you ride Domino." Dana patted the neck of her mount. "She's the oldest horse on the ranch and she wouldn't break into a trot if there was a fifty-pound sack of sugar cubes at the end of the road."

Erin recalled a harrowing ride over Arabian dunes on the back of a thoroughbred dromedary. What was intended to be a harmless photo op escalated into a bone-jarring race with another camel ridden by a professional jockey.

"Honey, I know a little something about being bounced around on the back of an animal. And even though Domino seems perfectly calm to you, with my sore pelvis, I'm afraid she'd feel like a bucking bronco."

"I gotcha. My backside and thighs hurt something awful the last few days but today, not so much. I'm going to try to help Daddy bring in a couple of strays this afternoon."

"That's what I hear."

"It's our last chance since I have to start helping with the arrivals tomorrow."

"Your Aunt Becky said she'd drive me out in the truck to meet y'all so I could shoot you in action. We'll put together an album to show your friends back home that you're not just a pretty face."

Erin gave a thumbs-up, something she would never do in the Middle East where it represents the supreme insult. Dana returned the affirming gesture as she responded to a shrill whistle from Daniel signaling she should join him.

On the other side of the ring, he worked with her on the proper twirl and toss of the stiff lasso. Erin gathered her camera and moved to the edge of the wooden fence to record their practice. Dana picked up the skill easily, the lasso flying in a smooth arc toward a target fashioned from a sawhorse and the sun-bleached horns of a bull. Erin caught every nuance of motion through her lens. A broad smile interfered with the squint of her eye as she endeavored to photograph the father and daughter work team.

It was such a pleasant scene that she let the camera hang around her neck so she could train both fully healed eyes on the action.

"Don't you get bored always bein' an observer, Erin?" Jake came to a stop beside her. He hooked one boot heel over the lowest board of the fence and rested his arms on the highest. "Wouldn't you like to engage once in a while?"

She chuckled at his rude but fairly accurate commentary on her life and angled her head toward the sling that supported her right arm.

"If this isn't 'engaged' enough for you, I don't know what is."

In apology, he dipped his head and touched the brim of his dusty work hat. "Sorry, that came out all wrong."

"On the contrary, I think you said exactly what you intended. Just like you do every time you insult Daniel."

"I beg your pardon," he took umbrage.

"Come on, Jake. You just strolled over here and dropped the hammer on me. Too late to pull punches now, don't you think?"

He nodded, ruddy streaks beginning to crawl above the collar of his denim shirt.

She continued. "I'll admit it, you're right about me. I've spent most of my adult years documenting the lives of other people instead of living in the moment myself. But at least I'm not afraid of physical peril."

"Neither is a rodeo clown and he gets the credit he deserves, too. But he'll never know what it is to sit on the top of a Brahman for eight seconds unless he crawls out of his barrel and climbs into the pen with that bull."

"Ouch!" She exaggerated a flinch from the sting of his words. He'd hit her sore spot, again. "That was the most insightful punch anybody's ever landed on me."

"You said not to pull any," he drawled. His face was fully engaged in a warm flush. Though the morning was still cool, a droplet slid from beneath his hat to his jaw line.

"If I'm the one on the hot seat, why are you sweating, Jake?"

He slanted a look at her from beneath the wide brim. "It's an old gut response. I break out in nervous heat anytime I expect I have a switchin' coming."

She shook her head to allay his concern.

"Let me repeat, *you're right*. My side of the camera is the safest place for me. I figured that out a long time ago and though I'm not likely to change, it never hurts to reweigh the odds once in a while."

"As long as you keep it under consideration. Even a blind hog finds an acorn in the woods now and again."

She grinned at the mental picture his words had painted. "Is that your way of saying that if I keep an open mind, I might eventually stumble onto something?"

"Good lookin' *and* smart. I expect being around you keeps my kid brother on his toes."

"Speaking of your brother, why do you always have a zinger queued up when Daniel's around?"

"I wouldn't say *always*."

"Only every time you speak to him. In the few days I've been here, I've heard you twist the blade on Daniel's career, where he lives, where he went to school, how he sits a horse, how he shoots a gun. You name it and you've criticized it, Jake."

"That's just how brothers carry on. It's pokin' fun, is all, and he knows it."

"I don't hear him laughing, do you? And Daniel doesn't dish it back, either. If you think about it for five minutes, you'll figure out it's not right to treat your only brother that way."

"I will?" Jake asked.

"Yep, *'cause even a blind hog finds an acorn in the woods now and again.*"

He snaked a long arm around Erin's shoulders and gave her side a light squeeze.

"I hope you come to your senses and decide to stick around, girl. It might not be a fancy family, but it's our family and you'd be a prize-perfect addition."

With her eyes downcast, she studied the pair of well-loved women's boots Tina Sue had been happy to loan. Erin had just experienced her first altercation with a family member in over twenty years. And it hadn't erupted into violence or ended in name-calling.

Maybe the Stablers were on to something.

And maybe Erin needed to take the first step toward finding the sister and brother she'd been separated from all those years ago. It had been on her mind constantly since she'd first looked into Dana's eyes. Alison would be thirty-seven now.

Would she still blame Erin for their mother's death?

Chapter Twelve

"I appreciate you dropping everything to drive me way out here."

Erin was grateful for the smoothness of the ride. The heavy-duty wheels absorbed all the dips and bumps as the old work truck cut straight across the expanse of pasture.

"Don't mention it." As always LaVerne selflessly shrugged off gratitude. "Becky was tied up with the camping assignments for the contestants. Heaven forbid we park the motor home of last year's third-runner-up for pork ribs right beside the beef brisket winner. Cook-off champs are a clannish bunch and they like to keep company with their own kind."

It sounded like a joke, but since LaVerne didn't crack a smile, Erin kept her amusement to herself. Maybe the staging of grills and smokers was the barbecue world's way of jockeying for position.

"Besides," LaVerne continued, "I knew I could drive to the spot in less time than it would take to give directions. Our herd has been hidin' their calves in the same ravine for forty years."

"Why do they do it?"

"Natural instinct to protect their young 'uns, I suppose. The crazy part is the heifers are safer in our branding pens than they are out here with the coyotes. But cows are too dumb to figure that out, so rounding 'em back up has become my boys' bailiwick."

"How about the girls? They seem capable."

"Oh, yes." There was a grandmother's delight in her voice. "They can ride and rope as well as their daddies could at that age. They've been a lot of help on the ranch. Even Dana does a pretty fair job these days. I'm proud of all my girls."

"I'm sure they appreciate hearing compliments like that, especially from you."

LaVerne studied the terrain, downshifting to steer around jutting rocks. Erin kept an eye on the older woman who seemed to be considering the conversation as well as the ground ahead.

"You *have* told them exactly what you just said to me, haven't you?"

"Now that you put me on the spot, I'm not so sure."

"LaVerne! Why would you share your feelings about your beautiful granddaughters with me, but not with them?"

She swiped a hand in Erin's direction. "Oh, they know. I don't need to say the words out loud."

"May I ask you a personal question?" Erin had a hunch about something and wanted to be certain.

"Why sure."

"Were you the only girl in your family?"

"That's a fact. I was the oldest of three kids."

"Were you close to your mother?"

LaVerne shook her head. "Mama favored my brothers. Neither of us minded much when I moved away, though it aggravated her to lose her kitchen help." She chuckled at the memory.

"So, you're probably not much like your mother."

"Right again. I've tried to treat all my kids the same."

"So they don't feel shortchanged?" Erin asked.

"Exactly."

LaVerne pulled the truck to the edge of what Erin judged to be a shallow canyon. On the far ridge she spotted two figures on horseback. Dana stood in the stirrups, with a lasso in her hand. Thirty feet away, a wayward Angus calf was under the watchful eye of a border collie.

Erin slid the camera strap over her head and prepared to descend from the cab of the truck. She thought of her conversation with Jake only hours earlier. He was right. These were moments she was meant to seize, to engage and not merely observe. Before she pulled the door handle, she turned back to LaVerne.

"Thank you for helping me share this experience with Dana. I've lost a lot of time with—" Erin stopped, considering how to finish the sentence. "I've lost a lot of time with my daughter. I wasn't there to encourage her when she walked, or applaud when she rode a bike or grimace when she got her eyebrow pierced. But I'm here today to tell her how much this means to me. I won't assume she knows I'm proud of her without hearing me speak the words."

"Bandit, stay." Daniel's command stilled the collie from its work circling the calf. The huge quarter horse beneath Daniel shuddered with anticipation, ready to sprint if the calf took off. "Quiet, you two. Let Dana and Domino get this one."

With her boots braced against the stirrups, Dana stretched tall, swung the lasso in two full circles above her head and tossed the lariat exactly as they'd practiced. The loop wobbled as it arced but settled over the calf's head. It bawled, dipped and pulled against the lasso, successfully tightening the rope secured to Dana's saddle horn.

"Well done, butter bean!"

"Nothin' but air!" She returned his excited grin.

"Okay, keep the rope tight and finish the drill."

Bandit sprang to life yipping at something that caught his attention on the top edge of the ravine. Daniel squinted against the sun. His heart thumped hard at the sight of Erin in jeans and cowboy boots. The camera blocked her face as she gracefully shifted side to side recording Dana's victory.

As a thought registered in his mind, it crossed his lips.

"I love you," he whispered aloud. The wind caught the inaudible words and swept them toward the open range along with the relief Daniel felt at having spoken his feelings if only to himself.

Erin's head snapped up. She took two steps backward and froze. Daniel's gut lurched at the thought of what might have distracted her. Snakes were plentiful and this rugged territory was their home. Rattlers didn't go looking for trouble but jumping one could produce a lightning-fast, deadly attack.

She didn't back away or turn and run. She let her camera rest on the strap around her neck, folded her arms across her chest and the way she tilted her head to one side, he'd swear she was smiling at him.

Daniel hadn't been caught red-handed at anything since he was a boy. But in a brief moment of chagrin, he realized he'd just been busted at the cookie jar. Through her telephoto lens, Erin had undoubtedly witnessed the words that trespassed his lips. Though it was impossible for her to hear his *I love you,* she must have seen it. He could feign ignorance or he could pretend the declaration was meant for Dana. But now the words and the truth were out. At least for him, for all the good it would do.

He'd never completely given up on his family. Always hoping there might come a day when they'd be reunited. And now he'd fallen in love with his wife all over again. While he couldn't exactly shout it from the rooftops, he wouldn't be ashamed of it, either.

Lord, Your Word says a man and woman become one when they marry. You desire for families to stay together in whatever form that may take. Please guide us back into Your perfect will.

"Daddy, look! It's Grandma Verne and Mama."

There was no mistaking the pride in Dana's voice as she made the unconscious leap, referring to Erin as her *mama.* Full as his heart was for Dana, a stab of trepidation took his breath. Both of their lives and now their hearts were invested in Erin. Daniel prayed it was not a bankrupt situation.

LaVerne waved and called from a distance too great to make out her words. She motioned in the direction of home and turned back toward the truck.

"Pull your hat tight for the ride back," he cautioned

Dana as they began the climb out of the ravine. "I got that old Resistol twenty-five years ago but it's still in pretty good shape. I don't want to have to chase it across three counties when the wind whips it off your head."

"How do I look, Daddy?" She fanned an open hand at the view of herself on horseback, a submissive calf to show for her efforts.

He winked at the second love of his life. "Like a pro. And your mama caught it all on film, so let's go take a look."

As the days went by, Daniel couldn't help but notice things were different. The fund-raiser tended to bring out the best in the family, but there was definitely a change this time around.

Like always, Jake was busier than a one-armed paper hanger. But no amount of work had ever before kept him from any opportunity to land a punch in Daniel's ribs. In recent days the low blows had become surprisingly few and far between.

LaVerne was up to her eyeballs cooking eighteen hours a day for the twenty-some-odd people who were in and out of her kitchen for every meal. Even so, she could juggle food prep, keep the sink clean, the pantry stocked and still find the energy to feed and lecture the Third Infantry if they marched up to her back door. But she'd become comfortably quiet, seemed content to hold her tongue and let Becky be the bad cop of the house.

Most different of all were the five girls. When they weren't about their chores, they were underfoot in the big kitchen abuzz with the drama of school, boys and pop culture. They chatted freely within earshot of their grandma, only clamming up when Becky strode through the house in search of something Jake needed. It seemed to Daniel that anytime he went looking for Dana, he found her at the kitchen table in stocking feet, her boots dutifully parked beside the door. Fitting in with her country cousins and accepting LaVerne's rule seemed like less of a chore now that her grandmother had loosened the purse strings on praise.

"I don't understand it, but I sure am grateful for whatever caused it." Daniel confided to Erin the night before the Barbecue Bonanza got under way. They enjoyed their new evening ritual of coffee under the stars while they swayed back and forth in the creaky old glider.

"Your presence has got this bunch on their best behavior."

"You exaggerate."

"No," he insisted. "Under normal circumstances, there's generally some hollerin' and fussin' going on. Not violent or mean-spirited, mind you. But around here, we've each been known to raise our voice to get a point across. And with this many women under one roof, there's gonna be at least one hissy fit a day.

"A couple hundred campers will pull in here tomorrow and by the weekend, if the good Lord's willin', another thousand will show up to eat. My family should be strung tighter than a mile of new barbed wire instead of acting like Santa's on the way."

"Daniel, stop analyzing and enjoy it. Focus on the peace of the present day. The Bible tells us tomorrow has enough trouble for itself, right?"

"So that's how you do it? You just deal with each day as it comes."

She nodded. "It started out as a survival technique but I've learned to be at home anywhere, even in a war zone."

Of course you have, he thought. *What I wouldn't give to have you stick around long enough for me to erase the tragic reason for those lessons.*

"Well, tomorrow this place won't resemble a war zone as much as a national sporting event. There will be motor coaches and trailers vying for position, folks tailgating, cookin' all-nighters and plenty of music. When you see how Jake transforms the covered stock pen into a judging arena, you'll think the home team is in the play-offs and he's the head coach."

She raised the thick coffee mug to her lips and shifted closer. He dared to interpret the movement as a snuggle but kept his hands occupied with his own hot drink. Though they hadn't spoken of it, there was a softer dynamic to their relationship. Even so, he'd kept a respectful distance.

"I'm getting excited about having some unsuspecting subjects for my photographs," she admitted, sounding like one of the teenagers. "Even the cows are starting to dodge me when the Nikon's around my neck."

"I know that's right! You seem to be everywhere I turn, so you're bound to have enough pictures of my ugly mug."

"Not even close," she corrected sweetly. "Besides, all this activity has been better for me than three months of physical therapy with Christina."

He motioned to the colorful sling Dana had fashioned for Erin from red bandanas.

"Even with that thing, nobody would suspect you're recovering from such a severe injury."

"God's been good," she offered up praise.

"He has, but you've done your part, too."

"Thank you, Daniel." The comfort of her small smile settled on his face. "Having goals always drives people toward success. I was sharing that with Dana just the other day when the older girls were talking about college. I hope you don't mind but I encouraged her to consider out-of-state schools if she settles on a music technology degree. There are some great production facilities in New York."

The casual comment from Erin was a sucker punch to Daniel's gut. Though he'd made his feelings about Dana's future amply clear, Erin had interfered anyway, and in a manner that put the heat on him if he and Dana disagreed.

"There are perfectly good schools in Texas where she qualifies for in-state tuition. But when the time comes Dana and I will make those decisions together as a family."

Erin's eyes widened as she suddenly realized she'd overstepped. "Of course, sure. But if she should choose out-of-state, I'll help with the cost. It's the least I can do."

She just kept diggin' that hole. He took another sip, counted to ten and then calmly spoke the words that had to be said. Sooner was better than later.

"Erin, you're right. Helping financially *is* the least you can do, but I've had college covered for years so we don't need your money. Dana deserves more than your least, she's holdin' out hope for your best. For a woman trackin' down a miracle, that shouldn't be so hard to get your head around."

She nodded, remained silent, didn't recoil from their close proximity. The defensive response he expected never surfaced. Instead, he got quiet understanding from eyes sending a message he couldn't interpret if his life depended upon it.

The more time they were together, the more confused he became, while Erin still seemed to know her mind. Her goal was never in question. Recovery was moving her closer every day to returning to the work she loved at World View. She'd be gone before they knew it and he'd have no one to blame for wanting more for his daughter and himself than Erin was capable of giving.

At best he had a couple more weeks with Erin and two more years with Dana. He'd pray for wisdom on how to deal with his losses as they occurred. But right now he would do as Erin suggested, focus on living day by day.

He stood and stretched out his hand. "We'll work through that when the time comes."

Though she was no longer physically dependent upon it, Erin accepted Daniel's help by taking his hand. As his warmth connected with the chill that had overcome her, she said a silent prayer for courage. Daniel was a straight shooter, said and did what was on his mind so you knew where you stood.

It was time she returned the favor.

Daniel hadn't made a single overture since he'd mouthed the words *I love you,* obviously unaware her camera was trained on his rugged face. For days Erin had been waiting for the opportunity to respond. If she didn't take action soon, she might never hear the words spoken intentionally.

So, before he could release her hand or she could lose her nerve, she took a step closer. Erin faced Daniel toe-to-toe, slipped both arms around his waist and pulled him near enough to feel the cool metal of his belt buckle through her T-shirt. She laid her cheek against his chest, breathing in the scent of laundry detergent and cinnamon.

Mmm, clean.

His body offered no encouragement as she persisted with her silent, one-sided hug.

Mmm, Daniel.

"Mmm, what?" he asked.

"Did I make that noise out loud?" *Good grief, I'm a loser!*

He took pity, brought his arms close and returned the light pressure of her embrace.

"Yes, you did. I suppose it has something to do with the way I smell after baking a dozen pans of apple cobbler for tomorrow."

"And you were very mean to deny anybody a sample." She used the pretend pout that seemed to work for Dana.

"The waiting makes it that much sweeter."

She tipped her head back. "I can't wait any longer, Daniel."

"For cobbler?"

"You're going to make me beg, aren't you?"

"Don't you think I deserve to hear it?"

"You most certainly do." She brushed the tip of her tongue over her lips and released a sigh. "Daniel, will you lean down here and kiss me?"

He hesitated. Not a sign it had been a good idea for her to step out on this ledge.

"Pretty please?" she asked

"Well, since you put it so nicely," he murmured, his mouth already hovering so close she could taste the warm sweetness of his breath. The urgency of his kiss stole what little reserve she'd been trying to hold on to.

This was sixteen years in the making. His palms smoothed upward on her low back, ribs and shoulders gently urging her closer. Daniel told her with his kiss what she hadn't yet heard in words.

This wonderful man, this committed father, this brave Texas Ranger, still cared for her.

Only the Heavenly Father understood how much she'd come to love Daniel in return.

He ended the kiss but kept her folded in his arms. Her cheek pressed close to the insistent beating beneath his ribs.

"Erin, when this madhouse settles down in a few days, we need to talk about our future. With Dana to consider, there's a lot to work through, but nothing we can't work out."

Her own racing heart plummeted. He was concerned for their daughter's future at a time when most red-blooded men would be entertaining selfish thoughts. Erin didn't know whether to applaud his parenting or stamp her boot at his foolishness.

But putting family first was the very essence of Daniel Stabler.

"You're right," Erin agreed. "There are probably a hundred details we have to iron out before I head back to New York."

New York? Daniel thought. She'd fit perfectly in his arms moments ago, but the very mention of the city made her back stiffen as if a gulf had opened up between them.

Of course she'd be thinking about getting back there. Even though life was a bare-bones existence when she was on the road, there must be glamour waiting in the city that never sleeps. She was in his home until she recovered enough to be on her own. She hadn't given him any encouragement to believe otherwise.

Until now.

He'd quit while he was ahead. Sort of.

"We can pick this conversation back up in a few days. Tomorrow's going to be busy for everybody, so let's call it a night."

He held the screen door for Erin who preceded him into the house. LaVerne was putting the last of her baked goods into individual containers for the sale that would start tomorrow.

"Son, would you help me finish up so we can have a private word?"

"Well, good night." Erin took the hint, continued down the hall and closed the door to his old room behind her.

Daniel knew the drill. He grabbed a sandwich bag and sealed six peanut butter cookies inside. "Why didn't you tell me you needed help? We could have been doing this with you for the last hour."

"No, I wanted to be alone and keep my hands busy while I prayed about how to tell you something."

He stilled. "What is it, Mama?"

She rinsed and dried her hands and motioned for him to follow her to her room. Beside the bed was the heavy carton of letters Erin's boss had delivered.

"You brought these home with you?"

She shrugged. "Well, Erin said I could read 'em and I never got around to it while we were still in Houston. I once wrote a note of encouragement to Betty Ford but other than that, I wouldn't know a fan letter if it bit me on the nose. So I was curious to find out what would make all these strangers write to Erin."

His mama had sorted the large box of opened envelopes and then stacked them according to subjects scribbled on pink index cards.

"Most of these folks try to describe somethin' in one of Erin's pictures that threw them for an emotional loop. The letters from the soldiers will just break your heart, Daniel. Those kids are so grateful to Erin for voluntarily being with them, capturing things they could never explain with words. I think there's potential here for a book."

"A book? Hmm, that's an interesting concept."

"But not what I wanted to talk about with you."

His mama was not one to mince words. She definitely needed to spit out whatever she'd been chewing on. Such discomfort and reluctance on her part was scarier than a Stephen King novel.

"Just tell me what it is."

"I'll have to show you."

She lifted a thick stack of envelopes that were still sealed, some yellowed with age and others appearing fairly new.

"There's no return address but they all have the same handwriting. The postmarks from San Angelo are spread over the last ten years."

"You didn't open them?" He could already see that for himself.

"I was afraid to do that for fear of who they might be from." She was rarely guided by restraint. Something was really troubling his mama.

"Like whom?"

"*Like a man.* What if there's been another man in Erin's life and you don't know anything about it?"

"If that was true, why wouldn't he know how to reach her in person and why wouldn't she want to read his letters?"

"That's why I brought them to you. To be honest, son, Erin doesn't want anything to do with all these letters. But they're too powerful to be kept in the dark. Or worse, destroyed. And this bunch from San Angelo is just down-right creepy. I'm putting them in your hands and trusting you and the Lord to figure out what to do with 'em."

Chapter Thirteen

Erin thrived on pandemonium. She found comfort amid racket and chaos.

That about described the arrival of a couple hundred contestants for the Double-S Bonanza. The carefully choreographed madness looked for all the world like a barbecue chef smack down.

All remaining soreness from her pelvic injury had subsided days ago. Constant walking had been the perfect therapy. And constant companionship had been the perfect medicine.

She'd pushed past her left-handed awkwardness. The limited dexterity of her right arm no longer made her self-conscious around others. In the months ahead, Erin would press her recovering limb toward a wider range of motion and work her uncooperative fingers to the bone with that gob of Silly Putty.

For today she was satisfied with her level of improvement and, to use Daniel's expression, she was champin' at the bit to get to work.

The fresh country air was charged with competitive pride and braggadocious friendship, qualities that motivated Erin to make the acquaintance of every single entrant over the two days it took them all to arrive and set up camp.

As a woman bearing professional camera equipment and a notepad, she was welcomed and regaled with the four gospels of barbecue sauce; vinegar and pepper, mustard, light tomato and heavy tomato. While each newcomer positioned the grill just so, Erin received a fresh batch of coaching on dry or wet rub and pork ribs versus beef brisket. She learned barbecue is a noun, not a verb. And anybody who thinks otherwise is likely to call home someplace north of the Mason-Dixon Line.

"See, way back in the 1500s it was the Spaniards who introduced the pig to the American Indians and the Indians showed 'em how to slow cook it with smoke. That's how authentic barbecue was first eaten and the good Lord meant for it to stay that way." The side of Charlie Mullin's Bluebird motorhome proclaimed him "Texarkana's Sultan of Smoke." Charlie shook his gray head, sorry for those who didn't have the facts straight. "Most folks have no historic connection to barbecue and they've been hoodwinked into thinking any piece of grilled meat qualifies. It's sad, I tell ya."

Erin had never been inclined to put captions with her photographs. But these slow-cooking foodies from every walk of life and all parts of the country had her chuckling and jotting notes. Before she knew it, Erin was mentally preparing the argument that would convince J.D. to support her in a fund-raising effort. If she was as popular as he claimed, maybe her reputation could sell a few coffee table books to help out the West

Texas Boys Ranch. With three boys of his own, J.D. would be an easy sell. While getting a book published wasn't his expertise, he knew the people who could make it happen.

By the end of the second day, her spiral notebook was full of anecdotes and the kernel of an idea was shooting up green sprouts. The more she put stories behind the pictures, the deeper the roots sank. It would be a new type of challenge, something within her ability. Something lasting that would help others.

Something she could share with Daniel and Dana.

"Erin, your phone's been ringing all afternoon."

LaVerne pointed down the hall where the cell was charging on Daniel's rolltop desk. It hadn't chirped in ten days and Erin didn't miss it one bit. Vegetable soup simmered in the kitchen, a nice change from the wood smoke of the camping area where lazy wisps of white snaked above the Double-S.

Alone in the bedroom, Erin slipped the camera from around her neck and lowered it to the surface of the desk. She rolled both shoulders and stretched side to side before settling into the high-backed leather chair to check for missed calls.

J.D. had phoned eleven times! Her heart raced from the surge of adrenaline that always accompanied an unexpected communication from the chief. Had the World View execs changed their minds? Had they decided to let her go after all? Erin took a moment to consider the possibility. Even though J.D. had repeatedly insisted her position was safe, nothing was certain in today's economic climate with jobs being lost right and left.

She relaxed against the comfortable chair that belonged to a confident and loving Texas Ranger. As Erin's pulse slowed, a strange calm settled into her body and spread over her spirit. She would be fine.

She bowed her head.

"Father, I'm no longer certain about Your will for my life. It always seemed clear that You were leading me to faraway places where no one else would go, to catch images another person might miss or avoid. I still feel like I have so much work to do, but boarding a transport to travel halfway around the world doesn't hold the appeal it once did. Lord, give me the grace and courage to accept whatever comes. Thank You for my healing and for Your mercy that is new every day. Amen."

She pressed the call return button and took a deep breath. He answered right away.

"Hey, boss. It's me."

"Well, it's about time." J.D. sounded anxious, but in a good way.

"I'm sorry to keep you waiting. It's busy out here and I've been getting to know the contestants."

"Out where? What contestants?"

Right. She hadn't told him about the ranch.

"I'm in Fort Stockton, Texas at Daniel's family home. They sponsor a big barbecue cook-off for charity. I'm helping out by taking some pictures."

"Wow! You were right all along about your recovery time. The suits upstairs will be pleased to hear it."

Erin noted the excitement in his voice, no indication of bad news at all. She was careful to keep a relieved sigh to herself, not wanting J.D. to be offended by a lack of faith in his word.

"So, what's up? Do you need me to coach somebody who's been filling in for me?"

"No, ma'am. I need you to come off the bench and get back in the game."

She sat upright, moved to the edge of the seat.

"What?"

"We have an assignment and you're the perfect person to handle it. It's the story of wounded troops forced to recover in the field. You'll understand their struggles and they'll identify with your injuries. Nobody will expect you to be full tilt already, so if you have to take it slow, we'll make accommodations. What do you say, Erin? Can you be ready to deploy to Iraq in ten days?"

Iraq? Ten days! Emotion squeezed her throat and choked any response. J.D. probably expected cries of elation but all she could think of were objections. This opportunity was what she'd aimed for, what she'd prayed for. This had to be confirmation that God was calling her back to embedded service. Or could it be His way of telling her to make a personal choice instead of laying the decision on Him?

She needed time to think.

"That's a tight deadline, boss." Even to her ears it sounded like an excuse. She tried for something closer to the truth. "I may have overstated my abilities just a bit. I wouldn't want this clunker arm of mine to put another person's safety in jeopardy because they're trying to cover for me."

"We'll support whatever capability level you're at, Erin. Having limitations will only endear you more to the troops and bring a deeper level of realism to your work. Our broadcast affiliates have been contacted about the possibility of shadowing you on the job and they are hot for this story. Not only will it get you back to the work you love, and help shine a light on the growing issue of wounded warriors, I daresay it may put you in contention for another Pulitzer."

The prize didn't matter. Any attention she could bring to her soldiers would be motivation enough.

But what about her reasons to stay put? She'd spent all afternoon dreaming about the good she could do for the boys' ranch right up the road. Boys who might grow into men and serve their nation at home just as Daniel was doing.

And what about Daniel and Dana?

Her family.

That's the way she thought of them now. But thinking it and living it were completely different. She'd survived a bumpy ride to come to this point in life and deserved time to weigh the impact of her decision.

"Can you let me get through the weekend? As I said, things are running a hundred miles a minute right now and I can't drop this on Daniel until the fund-raiser is over."

"Sure thing, no problem," J.D. agreed. "Let's talk first thing Monday. I'll send a car to take you to Midland where you can catch an eastbound flight. That'll leave plenty of time to get you ready to roll. You have your new equipment with you?"

"Of course."

"Perfect. That'll save a stop in Houston."

"I left a few personal items there." She was thinking

of her portfolio. Then a smile lifted her eyes as the football jersey crossed her mind.

"Daniel can ship anything important and we'll hold it here for you, like always."

Even without a few days to think it over, it seemed a fait accompli. If things could fall into place so easily, it must be right.

Just in case, she'd make the best of what time she had left.

People wrongly assumed it was an act of charity on Daniel's part to give up his vacation time each year to work the fund-raiser. The truth was he got more out of the experience than he ever put into it. Not only was he back home being spoiled by his mama and reconnecting with his only brother, he had the added benefit of time on a working ranch with Dana teaching her lessons she might never learn in the city. Throw in a Texas-size barbecue that helped fund a home for troubled boys and it didn't get any better.

At least that's how he'd felt before Erin came back into their lives. He'd worked around the clock to convince the world he could raise a child alone. Even before the day he pinned on the Ranger badge and outwardly declared his allegiance to the State of Texas, he'd made his personal priorities clear. He was on the job and available to his team 24/7.

Unless his daughter needed him.

He'd used his devotion to single parenthood to ward off well-meaning matchmakers and attractive suitors, and he'd successfully persuaded everyone he was happy.

Everyone except himself.

During his quiet time with God each morning, Daniel had begun to pray that one day his marriage would have another chance. He was beginning to feel like a man whose *one day* had come.

Throughout the hectic weekend of food preparation, tasting and judging, Erin seemed to be everywhere Daniel turned. Up close they exchanged modest touches and shy glances. From a distance her easy grin and wave let him know she was continually aware of his presence. Whether she was taking portraits of contestants or snapping candid shots of folks who'd driven down to the Double-S for the best selection of barbecue in the country, she was available to the family at all times.

And no job was beneath Erin. She helped at the cotton candy stand, carefully twirling and bagging huge wads of the sticky pink stuff as if it were spun gold. She did her time in the ticket booth, making change and guiding newcomers to the tasting tents. She directed foot traffic during the judging and even entertained anxious contestants with stories of strange foods she'd encountered in her travels.

To soften the effects of Dana's proud bragging, Daniel overheard Erin quietly downplay her accolades more than once. As expected, his daughter, whose fashion sense tended to ostracize her at these country events, made the most of her celebrity-by-association status. Dana printed news items off the Internet and brought along some of the magazines he'd saved over the years. When a West Texas cousin poked fun at her spiked hair or Goth clothes, she fired back with her new ammo. Properly impressed, most of them shut right up. Yep, Dana was in hog heaven.

Daniel could only guess Erin seemed to be on cloud nine as well. She was living in the moment like it was her last day on earth, always smiling and offering help, as if she couldn't get enough of their family and friends. She was a bottomless pit of questions as well as a tireless storyteller of exciting events in exotic places.

He was certain Erin was happy.

Still, something in Daniel's gut said it was too good to be true. A comment from her first night in Houston played over and over, a sound bite stuck in his head.

"As soon as I can physically manage on my own, I'll get out of your life." She'd never recanted that promise. And one kiss did not a new promise make.

Seeing her in action this week left little doubt she was able to manage most things on her own. Independence was second nature to Erin, so she had to be considering their circumstances, thinking about her next move. Was she trying on life as a family woman, cloaking herself in the comfort it might offer? Or was she just making fond memories to salve everybody's hurt feelings when she left?

This time the devastation would extend far beyond his own heart to include each person she'd touched with her kindness and courage. But his loss would be the greatest because she would take away a piece of Dana's heart and Daniel's relationship with his only child could never again be exclusively theirs.

Confronting Erin now might burst their bubble of happily-ever-after existence, exposing the situation for the fake that it was. There was no win in that, only the possibility that forcing the issue would hasten the inevitable. Daniel prayed it was God's will that the fragile perception would one day become rock-solid reality.

But, just in case, he'd make the best of the time he had left.

Erin scooted over, happy to make room for Daniel to flop down on the colorful quilt topped with an old tablecloth that she and Dana had spread in the shade. Before them was a banquet of smoked barbecue to make Thanksgiving dinner look like KFC takeout.

"You two are gonna give me a heart attack."

They'd laid out paper platters of ribs, brisket, chicken and links along with roasted corn, baked beans, coleslaw and buttered biscuits. In the center of the feast, an empty popcorn bucket donated by the local theater awaited discarded bones that would be picked clean.

"There's enough fat here to send Goliath for a cholesterol check."

"Oh, hush." The back of Dana's hand thumped him on the forearm. "You're skinny as a rail to begin with and we're going to burn it all off when the cleanup starts, so dig in and enjoy."

For the next half hour the three exchanged more moans than words. They communicated through finger licking, lip smacking, eye rolling and head bobbing. Erin believed she'd come to fully understand the science and skill of barbecue in the past few days. Today she learned there was a sign language, as well. When the cardboard container in the center of their picnic was filled with bones, corncobs and paper napkins, Dana doled out much-needed moist towelettes. Then she leaned back on her elbows and breathed in the fragrant scent of wood-smoked meats mingled with natural outdoor aromas.

"On days like this, I understand why the cousins are happy out here in the middle of nowhere."

"I know what you mean." Erin nodded. "I get the same feeling in the Saudi desert. I can completely relate to why the Bedouin people wouldn't consider living any other way."

Daniel finished wiping his hands and made a two-point toss of his wet nap into the garbage pail. "As a man who's spent a lot of time in these parts, I prefer to be where I can rinse the grit out of my teeth and have it stay like that for days at a time. I'm just a big sissy that way," he drawled.

Erin loved Daniel's easy willingness to expose his need for creature comforts. He told her stories about car stakeouts that had lasted for days and takedowns that had morphed into wrestling matches. He was a cowboy at heart, but he had a special appreciation for hot showers and indoor plumbing.

"Well, big sissy, it's about time for the dessert judging. Shall we head over there to get in on the final tasting?" Erin asked.

"Oh, that's right!" Dana hopped to her feet and grabbed her father by the hand. She tugged with bull dog tenacity pulling him to the soles of his boots. "Come on, Daddy. Let's go see how your entry does."

"Aww, prizes don't matter. I'm fulfilled by the appreciation in my little girl's eyes when she's got a mouthful of warm cobbler and homemade vanilla ice cream."

"Nice try, but I know how much you want that blue ribbon," Dana insisted.

"What makes you say a thing like that?"

"Last Christmas I gave you a new kitchen calendar. Before you even noted my birthday, your wrote WIN FIRST PLACE—in all caps—across the dates for this week."

"Hmm, did I really do that?"

"Yes, Daddy." Dana giggled.

Erin enjoyed the sound. It was a sweet melody that Daniel had been hearing since the day their daughter's funny bone was first tickled. How many more precious moments had they shared, just the two of them? Daddy and baby girl, having and needing only one another.

"You run on ahead and get us a good spot in the judging arena," Daniel suggested. "Check to see if Aunt Becky saved us a seat. She's carried on all week about that sticky marshmallow cake of hers, so she's probably on the front row practicing her acceptance speech."

Dust kicked up from Dana's feet as the heels of her boots pounded the ground in the direction of the covered arena.

Erin walked close at Daniel's right side. He captured the hand she intentionally brushed against his. She longed for him to change their course, to lead her behind the barn where they could steal a kiss like high school sweethearts. Though he shortened his stride to match hers, he continued on toward the judging.

"You're having a great time, aren't you?" she asked, even though the answer sparkled in his eyes.

"I love doing this event with my family. Daddy used to donate whatever we could afford to the boys' ranch each year but it was never as much as he wanted to give. He would be so humbled to know the family funds a perpetual trust in his name. After all these years, the community still remembers Percy Stabler for something more important than cows. You'll see on our last night at the sunset service."

If J.D had his way, she wouldn't be there for the memorial service to honor the patriarch of the Double-S.

"Does it get any easier for you to leave the ranch as the years go by?" she asked.

Daniel slowed for a moment as he considered her question.

"Mama still complains, but it's not hard on Dana and me because Houston really is home for us. But this year, it's gonna be different because of you. Erin, in a short time you've made a lasting impression. It'll be tough on everybody when we say our goodbyes, so let's not dwell on that today."

They walked the rest of the way without speaking. Hundreds of animated voices in the distance absorbed the silence while Erin marveled at Daniel's comments, at his calm.

He was *expecting* her to go back to her old life and he wasn't even going to try to change her mind. Just as he had sixteen years ago, Daniel would respect and honor her personal needs.

The black-and-white terrors that had driven her at eighteen seemed light years away. At thirty-four, a myriad of colorful emotions bound her to those she'd once abandoned. It would take true courage to change the course of her life at this late date.

And according to her sister, Erin Gray was a coward.

Chapter Fourteen

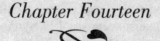

Jake sat at the head of the kitchen table with the fund-raising financials on a spreadsheet before him.

"After we pay the recycling and garbage services we are still above our goal by $2,200."

A cheer went up from those who'd gathered at the ranch house after the prizes had been awarded to celebrate another banner year.

"I think we can draw even more people next year if we have a big fireworks finale," Dana suggested.

LaVerne's family room erupted with objections. Jake held his hands up to silence the wisecracks.

"City girl, wildfires really tick off the neighbors, so we try to avoid a shower of sparks over dry grassland in the summertime."

"Good point, Uncle Jake."

"Every now and again…" He winked at Erin.

She was feeling like such a traitor. Here she stood in the midst of people who'd welcomed her unconditionally. They'd never raised the unanswered questions, hadn't once given voice to the criticism she surely deserved, and always made her feel part of the family. Whatever Daniel and LaVerne had said in preface to Erin's arrival must have been nothing short of life threatening. If comments had been whispered in private, they hadn't made their way into polite conversation. Not an insignificant accomplishment with a gaggle of young girls on the property.

And tomorrow at breakfast, Erin would repay their kindness by announcing she'd likely be gone before dark. These good folks deserved better, but she owed J.D., too. He'd given her a chance when she was nobody. He'd put his reputation on the line for her more than once and she'd always repaid him in spades. How could she do any less now?

"You're awfully quiet." Daniel settled on a bar stool beside her. With his blue ribbon hanging around his neck, he was so adorable she had to smile.

"Just tired, I suppose."

"You're in good company." They were all exhausted. "But everybody will be right as rain after they sleep till noon tomorrow."

"Noon?" Erin had been roused by activity in the kitchen before five every morning.

"Me and my big mouth." His handsome face took on the guilty look of a boy caught rifling Christmas presents on the twenty-fourth. Daniel glanced at Dana to see if she'd heard him. "I just blew the punch line."

"Then go ahead and tell me the joke."

"We always take a break the day after the competition wraps up. The campers can see themselves out the gate and everybody meets at Jake and Becky's for a late meal *with no barbecue on the menu*," he stressed.

"By early afternoon we have the ranch to ourselves again. Then we take it slow for a couple of days and look forward to the sunset worship the night before we leave for home." He checked for eavesdroppers and lowered his voice to a whisper. "The girls decided it would be a good prank to let you think you'd overslept. Now you're going to have to pretend or you'll get me in trouble."

Father, give me the words to tell Daniel the truth, she pleaded from her spirit.

Erin pressed her palm to his shirtsleeve and squeezed his arm as if to draw from his strength.

"I need to speak privately with you and Dana."

The grip of Erin's fingers on Daniel's forearm said his world was about to be rocked. The dread he'd been brushing away as wasted worry now settled heavy, a weight on his spirit. His Ranger instincts reminded him daily that the worst could happen, but he'd begun to hope Erin wouldn't let it come to that. He'd freely given trust though she hadn't earned it. Hadn't even asked for it. If his heart got crushed, there was only one person at fault. Himself.

He signaled for Dana to join them.

"Let's take a walk down to the bunkhouse so we can have a family meeting."

"What's this all about?" Dana quizzed her father as soon as the three excused themselves and stepped into the warm night air. "Did I do something?"

Though her face was in shadow Daniel knew her expression well. Like every child, her first reaction when anything went wrong was to assume guilt rested on her head. Though there was nothing to substantiate it, he knew his daughter had always felt somehow responsible for her mother's absence from their lives. Whatever was about to happen, he prayed Dana would not internalize the blame.

"Everything you've done this week has been perfect." He gave the back of her neck a tender squeeze. "I'm very proud of you. It's just we haven't had much time for the three of us, and Erin has something she wants to share."

Satisfied with his answer, Dana chattered about the day's events during the brief walk. Erin was silent, seemingly deep in thought. Or prayer.

"Here we are." Daniel flipped on the overhead lights and guided his two girls toward the room's oversized picnic table. He stepped first one boot and then the other over the bench and made himself as comfortable as a man can on a plank of wood. Erin and Dana faced him across the scarred surface.

"Erin, you called this meeting so tell us what's on your mind."

She inhaled loudly, they held their breath. She crossed her arms over her chest, they leaned closer. She closed her eyes and dipped her chin, they stared hard.

"Mama?" Dana mimicked the concerned tone Daniel used to encourage her when she needed to get something off her chest. "Whatever it is, we'll help you with it."

He ached with pride as his child reassured her mother, believing they could overcome anything together as a family.

Erin looked up through glistening eyes. At odds with the rest of her demeanor, a smile curved her lips.

"J.D. called a couple of days ago. They've offered me a new assignment. I'm going to photograph troops with injuries similar to mine while a video crew shadows me. It's a perfect vehicle to get the plight of our wounded warriors into the public eye."

"But that's great!" Dana gave her mama's hand an enthusiastic squeeze as she babbled on. "Are you sad because you'll have to go back to Walter Reed for a few weeks? We can handle things in Houston until you get home."

Erin's gaze met Daniel's and he knew where the rest of the story was headed. He took pity on the brimming bronze eyes.

"The assignment's in Iraq, isn't it?" He said the words she couldn't.

Erin nodded.

"For an extended period of time?" he asked.

She nodded again. "I've never gone over with an end date on the books. That comes with the territory. I'm there until World View reassigns me. And even with a draw dawn certain for next year, I feel sure they'll move me somewhere else in the theater of war."

Dana snatched her hand away as if Erin's flesh had turned molten. "You're not going, are you?"

"Honey, it's what I do. It's all I *can* do."

Dana slapped both palms on the table. "No, it's not! Look how easily you fit in here. You're not like me, all crazy and freaky." She ran her fingers through pointy hair, wiggled her many rings and tugged at the multiple piercings on her ears. "You're not only gifted with talent, you're *normal*. You can work anywhere, with anybody and be successful. You don't have to go to the other side of the planet for that."

"It's not so simple." Erin shook her head like there was no hope for another option.

"Then I'm going with you." Dana folded her arms, matter-of-fact, no further discussion needed.

"No, you're not," Daniel insisted, losing the battle to keep his voice calm. "You have two more years of high school and then college. After that you can call your own shots, but as long as I'm supporting you, I have the last say." He couldn't believe he'd just said that! It was pompous and dictatorial, and he might as well have thrown down the gauntlet.

"Fine. Then you won't support me. I do okay when you're not around, so what's the difference?"

He deserved that shot.

"Mama told me she was on her own when she was about my age and look how well she—"

"Stop it, Dana," Erin interrupted. "My situation was different and I would never wish that experience on another person. I had no choice. You do. Your father's right. You need to finish your education and if I'm back in the states by then, we can spend time together."

Dana looked straight ahead, her eyes not meeting Daniel's. Her lips pressed tightly, her head nodded.

"When will you leave?"

During the moment it took Erin to answer, no one drew a breath.

"Tomorrow."

Dana narrowed her eyes, looked first at her father and then her mother.

"So, this isn't a family meeting at all. It's just a private way for you to yank the rug out from under us without looking bad in front of the others. Well, I think it stinks like the manure that it is."

"Don't be crude," Daniel warned his daughter.

"Oh, so you don't have a problem with what she's doing to us, Dad? Your only concern is my language?" Dana jumped to her feet, a fist jammed on each hip. "Well, I've waited all my life to know my mama and I'm not going along with this. If I have to give up my home and my security to be with my family, that's what I'll do."

"*The Stablers* are your family," Erin softly reminded Dana. "They've been here for you all your life and they've earned your loyalty."

Her young shoulders slumped. A moan of defeat escaped her lips. "That's just it. I know my daddy's family. But I need to know the other half of who I am."

Dana scuffed the floor as she dragged her feet toward the door. She turned the handle then looked back at her mother.

"If you aren't here to teach me, who will?"

Erin felt the door beginning to close on her choices as it slammed behind Dana.

"I should never have come," Erin muttered certain Daniel must feel the same.

"To Houston or Fort Stockton?" His voice was strangely soft, but she could see the anger flex in his clenched jaw.

"Anywhere inside the borders of Texas. I know God doesn't make mistakes or I'd think my birth here was a mix up. As soon as I crossed outside the state line, for the first time, my life finally started to look up. I shouldn't have come back," she repeated. "There's nothing here for me and the people I love but pain."

Daniel moved to her side, sat down and folded his hands on the tabletop. She longed to feel his arm around her, to lean into him, to give into him. But give into what? He hadn't asked her for *anything*.

"Don't be absurd. The pain has nothing to do with the geography of Texas. It's all about what you keep buried up here." He tapped a fingertip to his forehead. "And even more about what you have growing in here." Daniel pressed his hand to his heart. "Erin, you can keep runnin' from it, but the real baggage is stuff that stays packed and can't be left behind. It'll be with you wherever you go until you deal with it. Why won't you trust me to help you?"

She closed her eyes against his words.

He took her chin in the crook of his finger and turned her face, forcing her gaze to meet his. She'd once stood at the breathtaking peak of Kilimanjaro. But in this rustic cabin in West Texas she saw the sparkle of forever in the golden flecks of Daniel's dark eyes. The comfort that stole over her was the same she'd felt at eighteen when she'd shared the secret of their pregnancy with Daniel. Without hesitation he'd declared he wanted her and their child forever.

"You're a brave lady, not afraid of risk," Daniel whispered. "How can I convince you to take a chance on us? The lifestyle may not be exotic but there's a lot to be said for being a Texas Ranger's family."

She couldn't think and yet her mind was crowded with thoughts. Daniel loved family above all things and a wife was his missing element. Was this his way of filling in an empty blank, closing a circle where she'd created a gap? Daniel would do anything for his daughter, and Dana was desperate to know her mother's history. He'd be meeting his child's needs but he'd never once confessed his own.

And what about Erin's needs? As Dana had pointed out, Erin was blessed with a gift for freezing a moment in time. She was free to go anyplace, was able to blend in anywhere. She could catch the unexpected because it never knew she was hovering nearby with her Nikon. Maybe the miracle that had eluded her was just another snap of the shutter away.

She still had so many photos unfinished in the lab and in her head. Someday she would slow down for that work, but right now God's purpose for her seemed to be 10,000 miles away.

"What do you say?" He wrapped his arm around her shoulders. "Will you give it another try?"

Will you give it another try?

Daniel's choice of words amazed her. Was he asking her to spend a lifetime with him or pull the handle of a slot machine? Being part of a family wasn't something she wanted to "try" like a new recipe. If she ever traveled that road again, there would be no turning back.

And "for keeps" is the only way Daniel should be willing to accept her.

Slowly, Erin shook her head. "I just can't deny God's hand in this opportunity. I think it's obvious what I'm supposed to do."

His skin burned where their bodies touched. He pushed away from the table and stood, knowing the same anger Dana had felt moments before. He paced a few steps away putting space and reason between himself and the woman he was suddenly desperate to keep in his life.

"I completely disagree with you. God brought you

home from a war on another continent, barely alive, afraid of the very word *family*. But look at us today. We have the choice to start over again. That is the obvious evidence of God's hand showing us what we're supposed to do."

She shook her head. "You don't know that for sure."

"Yes, I do," he insisted. "And I'm asking you to give it a couple more days if only out of respect for me. If you still feel you have to leave, I won't try to change your mind."

"J.D. wants to send a car for me tomorrow because—" she began to protest.

Daniel blocked the rest of her sentence with one palm outward before his face. He swallowed down the emotion rising in his throat, when what he wanted was to scream like a barn owl and smash his fist into the cabin wall. But losing control was not his style. It would give Erin the excuse she needed, and it would seal a fate that was never meant to be.

He exhaled to relieve the pressure of frustration in his lungs.

"With all due respect to your employer, I don't give one hoot in Jalisco about what J.D. wants. You and I and Dana are all that matter right here and right now. You said you could never repay us for being by your side all those days when nobody thought you'd make it. Well, now you can. Give me one more day of your life, Erin. Promise you won't make any decision for twenty-four hours."

He went for the takedown. "Promise you won't run out on us again."

Chapter Fifteen

Erin awoke at daybreak to a quiet ranch house, just as Daniel had predicted. But the silence had nothing to do with being punked by the girls. Erin's announcement the night before hadn't merely set a pall over the house, it had turned a celebration into a wake.

With Dana's upset so obvious, Daniel felt it was best to tell everyone the truth. "Erin has been offered an assignment and if she accepts, she'll be leaving in a day or two."

The noisy house emptied soon after.

In a loaner pair of red fuzzy slippers, Erin padded into the spacious common room. The aroma of freshly ground coffee and slats of sunlight across the pine floor welcomed her approach.

"I didn't expect you to be up for a while." LaVerne leaned on her elbows at the kitchen counter looking every day of her seventy-some-odd years.

"My arm ached all night. I thought a mug of strong java and one of your oatmeal raisin cookies would make a good chaser for my Motrin."

"Are you sure it's your arm and not your heart that's botherin' you?" LaVerne leveled an assessing look at Erin.

"Point well-taken." She busied herself with the old percolator, careful not to dribble on the tile countertop.

"Daniel left a note for you." LaVerne pointed to a white envelope on the table. "Said he hopes to be back this evening, but it may be tomorrow."

Erin felt a fresh stab of pain at the mention of Daniel. Maybe it hadn't been her injury keeping her awake after all. At least not the injury to her arm. She reached for the note, tucked it into the pocket of her robe and turned toward the back door carrying Daniel's favorite Hopalong Cassidy mug.

"Erin, when you come back inside, would you mind giving me a hand with something in my room?"

"Of course, I'll be glad to help."

Erin closed the screen softly. It could bounce off the hinges and never bother her daughter as she slept upstairs with the covers over her head, nothing but points of purple sticking out to give Dana's identity away. Funny, such a thought wasn't even a wrinkle in Erin's mind a month ago.

Not ha-ha funny. Sad funny.

The old glider, built to be quiet for two and complain about one, creaked beneath her weight. She sipped carefully, thinking of Daniel's way of blowing the coffee's surface each time it came to his lips.

His lips. The only ones she'd ever known.

She fished the envelope from her pocket and lifted the flap.

Good morning, Erin. I'm sorry to ask you for your time and then leave unexpectedly. But I had no option other than to follow-up on an anonymous lead. The window of opportunity is short and letting it pass could have dire consequences. I should be back by supper but it may be tomorrow. I would appreciate your understanding and your prayers. Much love, Daniel.

Of course, she'd pray. The criminals who trafficked illegals from Mexico into the U.S. were tantamount to animals. They were without conscience or morals, sacrificing human life as if it had no value beyond the money they extorted like bus fare.

She read the note a second time. He'd chosen his words carefully, probably imagining her reaction. She had every reason to be aggravated and insulted. He'd put the importance of his work over family only hours after he'd insisted she put her deadline on hold for the sake of the three of them.

Was this the way it would truly be in their home? Do as I say but not as I do? Was he talking a good game and then bending the rules for his team?

Her fingers brushed away a strand of hair along with the thought. Daniel was the most honorable man she'd ever known. At a time in her life when she'd been most vulnerable and alone, he'd been her rock. Twice.

She owed him the benefit of any doubt. But mostly she owed it to Daniel not to doubt him at all.

The chirp of her cell phone was muffled in the folds of the nubby chenille robe. That would be J.D. expecting her answer.

"Good morning, boss."

"Hey, kid! I can have a car there in three hours and

with only one connection, you can be in New York by nine o'clock." He paused to snicker to himself. "Aleutian standard time."

"I need another day or two, J.D."

"You don't say." The words echoed only mild surprise. "Things going that good or that bad?"

"I'm not even sure how to answer."

"Then it's best not to answer, yet. I have confidence you'll do what's right for you."

"That's just the problem. It's not about me anymore. There's Dana to think of now."

"What about Daniel?"

"For Dana's sake, he'd like me to stay. But I'm not sure that's the right reason to change the course of everyone's lives. Dana will leave home in a couple more years and then what?"

"Then you have a husband to share your life with. I know you feel like you've lived a lifetime already, but you're still a young woman, Erin. If you decide to live stateside, World View will adjust."

"You're not helping, J.D."

"Did you think I was going to argue with you?" He chuckled, as if the idea were out of the question.

"No, but I was hoping you'd at least give it a try."

"Kid, whether you choose the battlefield or a wheat field for your mission field, our Creator's miraculous hand will still show up in your work."

Erin rested her head against the cool metal of the glider as her eyes followed the lively flight of a Monarch butterfly. Then her gaze lifted to the jagged mountain peaks in the far-off distance. Whether from a few feet or miles away, the evidence of God's handiwork was in-

delibly stamped on this world. He didn't need Erin
Gray's help to prove a thing and it shouldn't take a
miracle to prove He'd always been in control.

"J.D., what made you say *miraculous?*"

"You haven't read any of those letters, have you?"

She shook her head. The silence was her answer.

"That's what I figured when I didn't hear from you."
There was wistful sadness in his words.

"They're still in that box in Houston," she admitted.

This time it was J.D. who was quiet. Erin imagined
him shaking his head at her stubborn refusal to read
what he referred to as her *fan mail,* a term she'd always
assumed was tongue-in-cheek.

"Before you make a final decision, I wish you'd have
a look at a few. Whichever fork in the road you decide
to take, I know what those people had to say will give
you a measure of peace."

"Thanks, boss. Can you buy me a few more days?"

J.D. paused for a moment. "Not this time, kid. I have
to put somebody on a flight to Baghdad in eight days.
It's travel tomorrow or not at all."

"I understand."

"And Erin—"

"Yes, sir."

"I'll still love you no matter what you decide. Even
more importantly, I believe Daniel will, too."

She slid the phone out of sight and crossed her left arm
over her eyes to soak up the tears that leaked unchecked.

Erin rinsed her cup and put it in the dish drainer.

"LaVerne? Do you need my help right away or can
I get changed first?"

"Come on in here," she called from her bedroom at the end of the hallway. "I don't plan to get out of my housecoat till it's time to go to Becky's and you shouldn't fret about it, either."

The door to the master suite was propped open with a red brick.

"Don't stump your toe on that thing," LaVerne cautioned. She sat in a leather recliner next to the bay window overlooking her back garden. "It's been there since the boys' daddy brought it in here thirty-five years ago for a temporary door stop."

Erin's mama had used a mason jar filled with pennies for the same purpose. That clear quart jar glinting with shades of copper flitted through the eye of Erin's mind. She felt the corner of her lips and her spirits lift at the brief image. How many other pleasurable memories had she buried so deeply that they could only surface through sensory association?

"What's all this?" Erin asked. A thick mosaic of white littered the quilt over the four-poster bed as well as the sofa and table positioned near LaVerne's comfortable lounger.

The older woman dipped her double chin and did her best to look contrite. LaVerne seemed to do very little that wasn't by design, so Erin figured the contrition was for show.

"I didn't get a chance to go through these back at Daniel's house and you didn't seem to want 'em, so I figured there was no harm in bringing 'em along. Each mornin' after my time with the Lord, I've been reading a stack. I've gotta tell you, Erin, these are hands down better than any devotional I've ever found. I apologize,

I'm not familiar with the pictures that go along with the stories, but I'm sure you will be and I'd like you to show me a few before you leave. I wanna see for myself the buried treasures these people all talk about."

Erin's laptop was right down the hall loaded with thousands of files. Which ones could possibly cause people to imagine hidden meaning?

"Here." LaVerne thrust a handwritten page at Erin. "Read this one first. It's my favorite, so far. I can't wait to see the angel."

Erin sunk down on a cozy window-seat cushion and began to read.

Dear Miss Gray,

Our newborn was only eleven days old when we lost him to crib death. Only another mother who's given up a child can understand the agony that gripped me and my husband. I needed to make something positive of the nine months I carried our little boy beneath my heart and the few days I held him in my arms. I needed assurance that his whisper of a life had been meaningful. I begged God to show me the purpose for my brief time of joy and my lifetime of loss.

My postpartum doctor visit was a nightmare. In the waiting room near me was a woman swollen with the promise of life and another beaming after the miracle of birth. My husband put his arm along the back of my chair and laid a magazine in my lap. Inside were several pictures by storm chasers. The photograph with your name beneath it stole away my heartbeat. The picture was taken from inside a darkened farmhouse. Beyond the window, the sky was black with thick clouds, the tip of a funnel dipped down as lightning split the air. It was a scene that would send everybody in our small town down into the cellar. But in that same moment of darkness, I caught a glimpse of peace. You have to look closely, and it took my husband a few moments to spot it, but then men and women rarely see things from the same perspective. The flash of the lightning rebounded against the window. The wings of a tiny, trapped insect were magnified in the glass, giving it the appearance of an angel, free from the bondage of life.

When my Bob finally saw it for himself, he was speechless but filled with understanding. God sent our little Robbie so we would never forget that the ties of earth are for a moment in time, but the glory of His presence in heaven is for eternity.

Erin's hand trembled as she folded the page. She remembered the old house in the Romanian countryside and the many pictures taken during the storm. She recalled one being selected for publication but she never noticed anything remarkable beyond the fury of the clouds.

"I'll be right back." She handed the letter to LaVerne and hurried the few steps to Daniel's desk and her laptop.

"Please let those files be here," she murmured aloud, not at all sure what had survived the transfer from her damaged hard drive. She switched on the desk lamp and tilted the shade toward the small computer as she tabbed through the folder labeled *Romania*. Her hand hovered over the mouse as the photo leapt to life. She tapped the zoom key until the window filled the screen.

"Oh, my goodness," Erin breathed, her hand reached forward as if to touch the smooth surface and find it three dimensional. "There it is. How could I never have seen it?"

"It's God's hand," LaVerne breathed over Erin's shoulder. She stood close, leaning down to see for herself. "You were there at *that* moment, to catch *that* bolt of lightning in *that* windowpane and it was the answer to *that* woman's prayer. It's a miracle." She shook her head, never taking her shimmering gaze from the monitor. "And the best part is, there are so many more."

"What did you say?" Erin's face snapped toward LaVerne for confirmation.

She pointed to her room across the hall.

"There are hundreds of letters in there and each one is different. People see things in your pictures that give them spiritual comfort. Some of the most incredible stories are from soldiers who were stationed near you, who witnessed the same things and places in person without recalling anything unusual. But in your pictures they see the shadow of God's hand, undeniably hovering, keeping 'em safe.

"Erin, you've got to match these letters with the right pictures and put 'em in a book. Just think how special that would be for Dana. But more importantly, you could be reaching thousands of people for the Kingdom who don't realize the glory and the proof of God all around us. Beauty's not the only thing in the eye of the beholder."

Erin remembered those freaky old pop-art posters from the '90s. You stared for a minute at what seemed like one thing, then your vision blurred and rebooted and your brain picked out something entirely different. The more recent picture-within-a-picture fad was a portrait made up of hundreds of tiny, unrelated photographs.

"LaVerne, that's a great idea and I promise to think about it. But the last thing I want to do is insult these people and my work by turning it into the latest craze at the mall."

"I have a hunch the more you read those letters, the less you'll worry about man interfering with what God is going to do in your life."

LaVerne opened her arms. Erin came to her feet and leaned into the comfort that only a mother can offer a child. Erin hadn't been hugged with such purity of heart in so long she'd forgotten how it felt. But she remembered how to respond. She rested her head against the shoulder of Daniel's mama and squeezed her eyes tight. For a moment Erin was a little girl again, before the grief of losing everyone she loved, before the loneliness of losing everything she knew.

It was a perfect parent-child moment that could only be better if she shared it with Dana.

"I think I'll go upstairs to see if my girl's awake yet." She gave LaVerne one more quick squeeze then turned to go.

"You think you can manage those steps?"

Erin nodded, pleased with another area of progress made on her own. "I've been practicing when nobody's around."

"Have you also been practicing what you're gonna say to Daniel? He loves you very deeply, you know."

Erin didn't acknowledge the question. She slumped one shoulder against the door frame, and fixed her gaze on the not-exactly-ruby slippers.

"I love him, too," her voice was little more than a whisper as she said the words for the first time in the presence of another person.

"You haven't told him, have you?" LaVerne's voice resounded with disbelief.

"No, ma'am."

"You know, the longer I live on a farm, the more I'd take horse sense over common sense any day," she huffed. She grabbed a blanket off the foot of the bed and made the soft fabric the target of her annoyance. Folding and slapping, folding and slapping, then shoving it into the cedar trunk beneath the window.

"Even the dumbest animal will show affection and love unconditionally if you give it the opportunity. But you take two perfectly intelligent adults, made for one another and blessed with a second chance, and they won't even speak their hearts. I just do not understand that."

"LaVerne, with all due respect, this is between Daniel and me."

"I beg your pardon, Doctor Phil, but you've been dispensing psychology on my turf all week long so I figured it was fair game to stick my nose in your business."

Erin's insides squirmed. She hadn't been taken to task in a long time.

"You mean our discussion about you and the girls?"

"Among others, yes. And as it turns out speaking your mind was the right thing to do because some good came from it. So I'm not gonna keep quiet either and then play woulda, coulda, shoulda when you go back to Timbuktu and my son goes back to living his life for Dana and the Texas Rangers. My Daniel's a good man and he deserves a full life. He won't ever have that without you, Erin."

LaVerne lumbered past and on down the hall to her quarters. A brick scraped the floor as it was scooted out of the way and the door shut with a thud.

The room was quiet with only the tick, tick, ticking of the bedside clock and Erin's breathing to compete with her thoughts. She prepared to do as LaVerne had suggested, practice what she would say to Daniel. As she closed her eyes to gather the words in her mind, an unexpected calm settled her nerves and a sense of purpose quieted her spirit. Comfort hovered over her like steam over a hot sidewalk after a summer shower and Erin knew what had to be said as soon as Daniel got back.

But just in case this moment never presented itself again, she would climb the stairs, slip beneath the comforter with her daughter, hug her close as only a mama can do and pray she'd be hugged in return.

Chapter Sixteen

A folded sheet of white paper fluttered from the wooden clothespin his mama kept nailed to her front door. LaVerne said it made it obvious for a visitor to spot the note. Jake said it made it obvious for a stranger to come on in and help himself since nobody was home and the coast was clear. But LaVerne had the last say, as usual. If a thief was desperate enough to drive way out to the Double-S to rob a small-time cattle rancher, he was welcome to anything he could cart away.

Daniel could still hear his daddy's voice, *"It's just stuff and stuff can't make you happy. It's the joy you add to the days of others that brings peace to your own life."*

During the silence of the three-hour drive to San Angelo, Daniel had thought hard about adding joy to the days of others. Then on the return trip, he prayed as never before that the plan he hoped would restore the joy to his family wouldn't backfire and send it crashing to the ground in flames.

"Everybody's up at Jake and Becky's." He relayed

the news of his mama's note through the open truck window. "I think it might be smart if you wait here and I'll bring them back in a few minutes." He'd had enough kindred confrontation in the past six weeks to last a lifetime, but he was pretty sure this would top it all. Best to find out privately.

"That sounds wise," Erin's sister agreed.

Alison Stone climbed out of the cab. She stretched the kinks out of her arms and legs before preceding Daniel up the six wide steps. He studied her from the back, recognizing her footfall, the tilt of her head, the square of her shoulders and the jangle of her concho belt and many silver bracelets. Dressed in expensive, handmade boots and a shirtwaist dress that resembled a crazy quilt there was no doubt about it. This woman with the thick auburn braid and dangling chandelier earrings was Dana's missing link. At long last, here was the family resemblance his daughter craved.

"The front door's always open. Make yourself comfortable and I'll be back as soon as I can."

"I'll just sit out here and enjoy the view." Her voice was calm. "And don't rush whatever you need to say to Erin. I've waited so many years for this reunion that a few more minutes won't make much difference."

Daniel heard lighthearted laughter drifting beneath the portico that surrounded three sides of his brother's hacienda-style home. The heels of his boots resounded against the stucco tile announcing his arrival before he turned the corner.

"Daddy's here!" Dana's voice blossomed with unusual excitement as she sailed around a smoothed cedar post and into his arms. There was urgency and fierce intensity in her hug.

"I should take unplanned day trips more often." He patted her back. "A man could get use to this sorta homecoming. What's goin' on, butter bean?"

The smiling eyes that met his were the spittin' image of the woman he'd left just down the road at LaVerne's place.

"Daddy, Mama wants to talk to you."

"Is that so?"

Dana nodded vigorously, her spikes wobbling. "I think she might have changed her mind about leaving."

His insides quaked. Had Erin reconsidered everything on her own, without his meddling in her personal life? And now, would his interference solidify the situation or cause a complete meltdown? Either way, life would play out. Pandora was waiting at the ranch house and there was no putting her back into the box now.

"Hey, you two. What am I missing out here?" Erin stepped into view. Her short bob, petite body and simple clothing were in stark contrast to her sister's colorful, southwestern style.

Lord, what have I done? Daniel's worry worsened. In the investigative unit of the Texas Rangers, he was known for rock-solid instinct. Had that sixth sense failed him when he needed it most?

He kept Dana secure with one arm and opened the other to Erin who stepped into their group hug.

"Well, this is sure a nice change from the last time the three of us were together."

"You've missed a lot today," Erin confessed.

"I'm sorry about that, but I had an opportunity I didn't dare pass up," Daniel apologized.

"I understand. I had several of those today myself." Erin's comment was mysterious.

Daniel noted the way mother and daughter stepped away from him but still clung together arm in arm. Something had definitely changed between the two and he was the odd man out. Dread crept up his spine.

"Dana, would you give us a few moments alone?"

"Sure," she agreed, ready to rejoin whatever fun she was missing on the other side of the house.

"But don't go far. Someone's waiting for us at your grandma's, so we need to leave in a few minutes."

Dana's brows pulled together, confusion and concern dampened her high spirits.

"It's okay. Don't worry," he assured her.

Yeah, like you believe that, a small voice niggled at him.

Erin caught his hand and pulled him farther away from the hearing of others.

"Did J.D. send a car after I told him not to?" Her eyes narrowed as if considering what punishment would fit that crime.

"No, it's not that at all. I had to drive up to San Angelo for an interview and I gave someone a ride back with me." He watched Erin's expression for any sign of recognition, but there was none. Alison confirmed there had been no contact between the sisters and their little brother since a family court judge had named them wards of the state nearly twenty-five years ago.

"So, you talked with J.D." Daniel leaned against the warm stucco of a decorative wall that surrounded the rambling house. She did the same, standing close enough for their shoulders to touch.

"Yeah, but we only spoke for a few minutes. Mostly I've spent the day talking about lots of things with LaVerne and Dana. And now, I need to share some thoughts with you."

Daniel wanted to enjoy the confidence in her voice. It sounded like she'd weighed the evidence carefully and come to a conclusion. But the truth was she didn't have nearly all the facts. Once she did her security would be shaken. And it would be his fault.

"Remember those letters J.D. brought to me?"

Daniel bobbed his head. His flesh burned where she placed her hand on his forearm below a rolled up cuff.

"I finally read some of them. They're remarkable stories and your mother gave me a wonderful idea for a book that would combine the letters and my photographs." Erin dipped her chin and teased a pebble with the toe of her boot before meeting his eyes again. "To tell you the truth, I'd already started considering a publishing project. I've got to believe the similarity of our ideas is more than a coincidence.

"Maybe Dana's right. Maybe I can retool my career and channel my ability in a way that doesn't require living on another continent."

Daniel swept off his Stetson and dabbed his brow with his shirtsleeve. The afternoon was warm, but he couldn't attribute his sweat to the weather any more than he could blame his churning stomach on lunch.

"What are you saying?"

Erin's eyes searched his face, her lips parted as she prepared to answer. He wanted to kiss those soft lips but deception was bitter in his mouth. Here was the moment he'd longed for, prayed for. And he couldn't concentrate for fear that whatever they wove together now would unravel within the hour.

"I'm saying if your offer's still open, I'd like to give us another try. Give family a try."

She was accepting the proposal he'd made the night before and with the very words he'd used to suggest it. And in that moment he knew just *giving it a try* was not giving it enough.

God required more.

They all deserved more.

Her smile was weak. She read his face and his body language, knew something was wrong. He couldn't put her through this any longer.

"As much as I'd like to celebrate what you just said, the moment's not right. Let's get Dana and head back to the house and then we'll make some decisions together."

Erin felt every accelerated beat of her heart through the throbbing of her right arm. She flexed and clenched her fingers to reduce the stress without respite. She ached low in her back, and her legs wobbled now that she was off her feet in the front seat of Daniel's SUV.

Medication would help the physical symptoms but there was no relief for the emotional pain she sensed bearing down on them. It began to form when she'd laid eyes on Daniel back at Becky's house and the foreboding had grown stronger with each breath.

Something was terribly wrong.

Daniel was an honest man. If he had a poker face, he

kept it in his desk at work. She didn't need a second opinion to know he was worried.

He must have regrets about what he said last night. Erin racked her mind for what might have gone wrong. *He's had all day to reconsider asking me to be part of their lives and he's decided it was a mistake.*

She could let him off the hook, give him an easy out, tell him she was flexible either way. But Dana was an arm's length behind in the backseat, tuned in to every word, every vibe in the vehicle. She too had grown quiet, knowing something was up with her dad.

LaVerne's big white house rose up a hundred yards in the distance. As they drew closer, Erin could make out a figure on the red glider. Dana leaned forward for a better look and the person stood, revealing a colorful, flowing skirt and boots.

It's a woman. Erin realized with a jolt. *Is that it? Has he reconnected with someone from his past?*

"Who's that, Daddy?"

"You don't know her, but your mama does. They haven't seen each other for a lot of years."

They passed the last forty yards in slow motion. The woman took several strides toward the edge of the porch, into the late afternoon light. It glistened like an auburn halo around her face and danced on her shiny jewelry. She stood with her arms folded across her chest, but there was no hiding the fullness of her hourglass figure.

Daniel pulled to a stop. The stranger was only a dozen feet away. Erin stared closely at familiar elements; the fair skin, the high forehead, the pointed chin.

The visitor removed dark glasses revealing her eyes.

Dana's eyes.

Alison!

Erin clutched her stomach, certain she would be sick in the floorboard. She was assaulted by little girl memories, long ago and deeply buried for the self-preservation of a nine year old.

She turned on Daniel. "Why would you do this? How do you even know?"

"Who is she?" Dana's voice matched the near panic in Erin's.

"My sister!" Erin choked on an anguished cry. She pushed open the door and settled her feet on the dirt road. Then she turned away from the house, marching in the opposite direction as fast as good sense would allow.

"Erin Elise, wait!" Alison shouted, her boots pounding the road, closing the distance between them as she caught up, put her hand on Erin's shoulder.

"Don't!" Erin twisted away. "Don't call me that and don't you dare touch me." She swung her right fist high to strike Alison. White-hot pain thundered through Erin's arm. Recovering muscles, weakened tendons and atrophied fasciae cried out. A gasp caught in her throat, her knees buckled, she folded at the waist and crumbled face-first into the dirt and gravel. The sound of Daniel's voice kept Erin from giving in to the luxury of a full-out faint.

"I've got you, baby." He was there, scooping her against his chest, cradling her close, whispering words of apology interrupted only by tender affirmations of love. He whisked her up the steps, through the house and into his room where he settled her with great care against the pillows. With her arm pressed close she took shallow breaths, squeezed her eyes tight and prayed she hadn't done permanent damage.

"Dana, get a warm washcloth and your mama's ice pack from the freezer." He barked orders and their daughter responded. Within minutes Erin's arm was immobilized with a sling and frozen gel pack and she'd gulped down the first pain meds since Houston. Her face was lovingly cleaned and Daniel applied antibiotic cream to the gravel scrapes. He murmured instructions to Dana in the hallway and then shut the door from the inside.

With her eyes closed beneath a cold cloth, Erin felt the pressure of Daniel's weight against the mattress. He eased close, slipped one arm behind her head and wrapped her carefully with his other.

"Baby, I'm so sorry." His voice was choked.

She rolled her head to the side. The cloth fell away and she was nose to cheek with the man she loved. Tears rolled in quiet streams from his eyes to his quivering jaw and then dribbled to the pillow.

"Why did you do this to me, Daniel?" It was a simple question requiring answers on so many levels. "I wanted to stay. I even thought about finding Alison on my own someday. The two of you didn't have to ambush me."

"It wasn't meant to be that way. She's been trying to reach you for years. There were at least twenty letters from the same child psychotherapist's office in that box. When I read them and realized who she was, I tracked her down and she agreed to come here. Alison wants to make amends with you and your brother. She couldn't defend you when you were only kids, so she's built her life around protecting children of family violence."

"My brother," Erin whispered.

"Alison knows where Heath is, but he refuses to respond."

"And our father?"

"He served over twenty years before he died of lung cancer."

"Alison told you about him?"

Daniel smoothed the hair away from Erin's forehead and pressed his cheek to hers. "I've known almost from the beginning, honey. As soon as I had access to confidential state files, I figured it all out. I had to so I could document Dana's family history for her on the remote chance that you never came back."

"Remote?" Erin shook her head. "All these years and you never gave up. How could you hold on to hope when there was absolutely no reason?"

"Let me show you." He extricated himself from their awkward embrace, crossed to his desk, slid open a small drawer and reached inside. He passed his right hand over his left and held it up for her to see.

Tears flooded her eyes but couldn't block her vision.

"Oh, Daniel. You still have your wedding ring."

"It's worse than that." He knelt beside the bed so his face was once again close to Erin's. "I still have our divorce papers."

"You mean you keep a copy like a souvenir?" She scrunched her face at the odd sentiment.

"I mean I have the *originals*." He mirrored her scrunched face. "I never filed them."

"What?" Her voice rose. "I signed those six months after I left."

"But I never finalized the divorce. Erin, in the eyes of God and the eyes of Texas, we're still married."

* * *

He'd confessed the worst there was to say. Erin may walk out on him tomorrow, but his conscience was finally clear. Daniel whooshed out a heavy sigh, his heart lighter for the release of his secret burdens.

"So, let me get this straight." The injured, emotional, medicated quality of Erin's voice was gone. An angry edge took its place as she ticked off her complaints.

"You've just brought the sister whose accusations have haunted me for twenty-five years into my daughter's life without my permission. They look like twins separated at birth and will probably get along like peas in a pod. Alison will undoubtedly share the story of our dear father who died in prison. And it's unlikely she'll leave out the detail that I hid in the pantry like a coward while he beat our mama to death. Then there's a brother out there somewhere who seems to have chosen to remain free of this curse. And since I tried very hard to do the same for a number of years, I for one will honor his wishes.

"And, last but not least, you and I are still married. *Technically.* Now tell me again how I'm not supposed to feel ambushed. These last weeks have made me want all the things I've protected myself and our child from— for most of my life. And now I will have those things, but by ipso facto and never by choice."

Daniel rose from his knees to his full height.

"That's where your train of thought just jumped the track, darlin'. Nothing about what you can have with me and the rest of this family is by default. It's all by choice. These circumstances are not a harmonic convergence of the universe. God brought us all together because this is where we belong. As a family we honor one another, but mostly we honor Him. And we do it by choice.

"I don't want you to stay for Dana's sake. She's sixteen years old and very capable of getting on a plane and meeting her mama anywhere in the world if that's what you two choose. And don't stay *or run* because of your sister. If you decide not to have a relationship with her, Alison will accept that just as she accepts your brother's wishes."

He reached for the battered old cowboy hat he kept on top of his reading lamp and clamped it on his head.

"And as for me, I only want you because you choose to be with the man you love. Hear that? The man you *love*. When I committed myself to you before God, I meant it. I deserve the same in return. If you can't give me that, then I'll dig out those papers and take them to the courthouse in Fort Stockton tomorrow. But make no doubt about it, Erin. You do have a choice. You *always* had a choice."

Before she could respond, he was gone. Slipped quietly through the door and pulled it closed behind him.

The cell phone buzzed. She was sufficiently medicated now to roll to one side and grab it off the nightstand.

"Yes, J.D." She did her best to sound normal.

"Hey, kid. Sorry, to bother you again but the plot thickens. The execs upstairs have another offer for you. There's a spot here in the New York bureau and if you want to live stateside, it's yours. So add that to your list of choices and give me a call in the morning. The clock's ticking."

Chapter Seventeen

Light rapping of knuckles on wood woke Erin from her medicated stupor. Beyond the sheer curtains, the sky was black. She'd slept for hours.

"Erin? May I come in?"

Alison. There was no running away this time.

"Sure." Erin flipped on the table lamp.

The door opened slowly as Alison stepped through. She'd been a striking girl and she was a stunning woman. For an instant Erin was grateful that Dana could see her aunt, to have an idea where her quirky beauty was headed.

Alison took the desk chair, her skirt fanned around her like the tail of peacock. She crossed her legs giving Erin a look at boots with "Ali" written in script across the leather shafts.

"Are you married?" For some reason it was the first thing Erin wanted to know.

"No," Alison replied. "I have the same fears you do, Erin. But it took a Ph.D. in psychotherapy before I figured that out. You protected yourself from the violence with distance. I built immunity by studying it. My patients are my kids and unfortunately there will always be an endless supply of them to fill my life."

"That isn't what I would have expected for you, but then it's been so long I don't even know who you are."

"Well, I know who you are from your work." Alison's voice was soothingly soft, probably a product of years spent working with damaged children. "From the first time I saw the name *Erin Gray* beneath a photograph, I knew it was you using Mama's maiden name. I've followed your career with great pride, little sister. I actually put together a scrapbook of every picture I've been able to find. They're incredibly spiritual. I call them my 'glimpses of God.'"

Once again, Erin was dumbstruck to hear she'd missed what others had seen. Was it the forest-for-the-trees syndrome, or had she merely been avoiding the obvious so she could continue to chase after phantoms? The constant running was exhilarating, but it was also tiresome.

"Erin, listen. I completely understand that my coming here was an unwelcome surprise for you. But I happened to agree with Daniel that today presented an opportunity we couldn't pass up. I'm leaving first thing in the morning and any future contact between us will be up to you. I won't force myself on you or Heath but my door will always open to both of you.

"And I'll respect whatever boundaries you need to set between me and your adorable daughter." Alison held up both hands and fluttered her bejeweled fingers. "There's no doubt we're sisters under the skin, but she's your child and I won't cross any line you need to draw."

Erin choked on a simple "Thank you."

"You're welcome, little sister. By the grace of God, I parlayed my neurosis into a lucrative practice and you channeled yours into works of art. He used the evil in our childhood for His good in our adulthood. I won't say I'd do it all over again, but I will say it's been an interesting ride."

Alison stood, shook out her skirt and gave a little twirl. Her bracelets jangled like a chorus of tiny bells.

"What do you think?"

"I think Mama would be very proud of you."

"Oh, Erin Elise, thank you for saying that." Alison crossed the floor and sat close on the edge of the bed. "I wasn't there when she needed me, so I've worked all my life to make up for it."

"I guess I have, too," Erin admitted. Silver clinked as Ali moved her hand to capture Erin's. "Every risk I've taken has been to prove I'm not a coward."

"Coward?" Ali's voice rose. "Why would you say that?"

"I hid. I didn't try to stop him."

"Baby girl, you were nine years old. And you didn't just hide, you protected Heath. If you hadn't taken him into that pantry with you, there's no telling what might have happened."

"But you called me a coward."

"And you have to forgive me. I was only a kid myself. One of the things I've learned about the mind of a child is that it's an amazing recorder but it's a terrible interpreter. You and I have hundreds of memories that need to be sorted out and put in their proper place. Maybe one day we can do that. It's your choice."

She stood, prepared to leave.

"Ali, do you remember that jar of pennies Mama used for a door stop?"

"I sure do. It was an idea you had for Mother's Day. She loved that gift." Ali smiled, waved and was gone.

Erin lay in the radiant glow of the lamp and the effervescent glow of her sister. She hadn't remembered where that big mason jar of pennies had come from, but Ali had. Her sister was right. There were too many memories to sort out alone. Maybe they needed to do it together.

Daniel sat by himself in the dark. His heart was heavy with the greatest sadness he'd ever known. He dug the heels of his boots into the porch to slowly rock the screechy old glider back and forth, a dirge for his soul.

"It's quieter with two," Erin whispered.

"Then come join me."

She settled close beside him. Without hesitation she rested her hand on his thigh and her head on his shoulder. If the roller-coaster ride they'd been on didn't end soon, he would have to go on blood pressure medication. At thirty-eight, he hoped he still had most of his life ahead of him. But the hammering and swelling and shrinking of the heart inside his chest were aging him prematurely.

"May I ask you a question?"

"Anything," he answered. There was nothing he wouldn't do, give or say to make the woman beside him happy.

"If you really meant *forever,* then why did you only ask me to *try?*"

He wrapped his arm around her and pulled her heart as close as he dared to his own. "Erin, honey, you're as skittish as a day-old calf. If I came at you with a branding iron, you'd kick me and run. I thought maybe I could draw you in with a range cube and then slip a rope around your neck. Or, better yet a ring around your finger."

Her left hand reached up to caught his. "You still have it on."

"Yes, ma'am. There's no use hidin' it from you now. Once you have your final say, I'll put it away."

"What if I say I want one to match it?"

"Forever?"

"And ever. Amen."

"Then I'd say that's easy 'cause it's in the same drawer where I've kept this one. They belong together. They always did."

"Just like us, Daniel."

Erin turned her face up to his. Her eyes glistened, her smile sparkled in the moonlight, her face was alight with joy, but there was more. She radiated the peace that only comes from living smack in the middle of the Father's will.

"I adore you, Erin. I promise to spend every day of my life proving that to you. With God as the third strand of our braided cord, we'll be strong enough for anything the future holds."

"Daniel, my love." She cupped his jaw in her palm, gently pulling him closer. When their lips were only a breath apart she whispered, "You waited for me. You prayed for me. You saved yourself for me. Tomorrow night at sunset will you reaffirm your vows with me in the presence of a Texas Ranger's family?"

"I will," Daniel answered, his voice filled with emotion, his heart bursting with love.

And then he answered her a second time, a forever time, with his kiss.

Epilogue

A ball of red-orange fire hovered above distant peaks sending streaks of gold across a canvas of azure blue. God's hand-painted benediction blessed the day and the western sky.

Erin tipped her head back to get a better look at the groom by her side. It was a moment she would cherish always and she gathered it to her heart, a precious memory she could examine again and again.

"Do you mind one more picture?" Daniel had never been more handsome. His eyes reflected the setting sun, his tanned face was alight with joy and peace. "I promise this will be the last one and then we'll go down to our reception."

Erin smiled and squeezed his hand where their wedding bands touched. "You've already given me the only promise I'll ever need. I'm content to stand here until your mama has every picture her heart desires."

"I hope you didn't mind such a whirlwind wedding," he apologized for the rush. "I know how girls dream of their special day. You got shortchanged the first time around and I don't want you to have regrets about today."

It had been head spinning to witness what the family had pulled together in twenty-four hours. But at the end of a hectic afternoon, everyone climbed a hillside to the arbor Percy Stabler had designed for his wife LaVerne some thirty years ago. Surrounded by loved ones, the wedding couple pledged their lives while standing beneath weathered crossbeams that had been hand-hewn by Daniel's daddy. The solid structure somehow made the family seem complete.

Then Dana joined them to read from Ecclesiastes, reminding everyone that a cord of three strands would not be easily broken. Their lives were entwined forever and nothing this side of heaven would separate them again.

Erin raised her hand to Daniel's face and traced the jaw that was every bit as solid as his faith.

"Regrets are all in the past, my love," she assured him. "God has plans to give the three of us a future and a hope and that begins today."

"My beautiful bride," Daniel whispered where only she could hear, his voice gruff with emotion. "You have made my life complete. Without you I would never have known the love in my heart at this moment."

"My amazing husband," she answered, standing on tiptoe to bring her face closer to Daniel's. "You taught me the very meaning of love when you brought me home, trusted me with Dana, invited me back into your family."

"It's where you always belonged. The circle was broken without you, Erin. But today we're whole."

"Smile, y'all!" LaVerne called before flashing a camera in their faces, catching the miracle of a Texas Ranger's family on film.

* * * * *

Dear Reader,

This is a story I have wanted to write since April 28, 2005 when a female soldier's photograph appeared on the cover of *USA TODAY*. A beautiful young redhead held her prosthetic right arm and stared proudly, if unsmiling, into the camera. The caption read:

A rocket-propelled-grenade attack in Iraq cost Lt. Dawn Halfaker her right arm.

My recent research on Ms. Halfaker indicates she has flourished in spite of her disability. In addition to earning a Purple Heart and Bronze Star, she earned the rank of Captain before retiring to become CEO of Halfaker and Associates, providing national security services for the federal government.

Our heroine in *A Texas Ranger's Family* was my small effort to honor all our Wounded Warriors, but particularly the women who share the dangers of the front lines. It is estimated that over 100,000 individuals have been wounded in combat since the war in Iraq began. I implore you as a Christian, do not forget the men and women who stood in harm's way to protect our freedom. Go to www.WoundedWarriorProject.org to learn more about how you can show your appreciation and support.

Until we meet again, let your light shine.

Mae Nunn

QUESTIONS FOR DISCUSSION

1. Do you see Erin as brave or cowardly for leaving her child in order to stop the cycle of violence in her life?

2. Do you believe a single father can raise and relate to a daughter successfully? Why or why not? How has Daniel's actions proved or disproved your thoughts on the subject?

3. Daniel has help from Abundant Harvest Church where he and Dana are well-connected. Is there a single-parent family in your church community that reminds you of the Stablers? Have you personally reached out to that family?

4. When Erin reconnects with Daniel and Dana there are sixteen years of unanswered questions between them. Could you have been as patient with Erin as Daniel and his family? Do you think Erin deserves their understanding?

5. Has anyone ever come back into your life after a long, unexplained absence? How did you handle the reunion?

6. Forgiveness is pivotal to the family's ability to heal and overcome past hurts. Christ commands us to forgive others so we will be forgiven. Is there someone in your life that needs forgiveness? Why or why not?

7. Erin is learning to live with a disability. How would you handle losing the use of your dominant hand? How do you deal with disabled people you encounter in your everyday life?

8. How difficult will it be for Erin to transition from her dangerous, nomadic world to life in the soccer-mom suburbs? What would you do to welcome her as a new neighbor?

9. LaVerne is a very special character in this story. Is she anything like your mother or your mother-in-law? If so, how?

10. Like Daniel and Jake, even the best of sibling relationships can be trying at times. Was there a situation with a sister or brother that was difficult? Describe how.

11. Where Daniel lived in a day-to-day world of reality and responsibility, Erin's lifestyle allowed her to live on the go, chasing her impossible dream. Which one of them do you feel was most comfortable in their own skin? Why?

12. Dana conveyed her identity confusion with Goth clothing, piercings and purple spiked hair. If your daughter or son brought Dana home for dinner, how would you react? Do you think Daniel was right to allow her the freedom to express herself in this manner? What was the most outrageous way you expressed your style as a teenager?

13. God's glory is evident in everyday life from the birth of a child to the majesty of mountains. But He also works in unexpected and mysterious ways we most need to experience His presence. Can you share a time when God moved in a miraculous way in your life?

Private investigator Wade Sutton plans to hightail it out of Dry Creek long before December 25. The town holds too many *unmerry* memories. Until he's asked to watch over a woman in danger, a woman whose faith changes him forever.

Turn the page for a sneak preview of
SILENT NIGHT IN DRY CREEK
by Janet Tronstad.
Available in October 2009
from Love Inspired®

Wade wished he had never come back to Dry Creek. Or, since he had come back, he wished people hadn't been so kind to him. Barbara making that cake for him was putting him off his game. And then Jasmine—usually he didn't have any trouble taking a tough line with a suspect. But then, he'd never been tempted to kiss a suspect before.

He watched Jasmine's back as she walked to the table. She was ramrod straight and angry with him. He knew he'd come on too strong, but it was either that or forgetting everything he knew about law enforcement and refusing to believe she could be responsible for anything.

As a lawman he had to consider all the possibilities, and it was hard to forget that Lonnie had been her partner. She could have sent him a coded message that in some way had helped him escape from prison, or at least given him an incentive to risk everything to get outside.

He wished he knew how to look into the heart of a person so he would know what Jasmine was thinking. Was she as innocent as she looked, or as guilty as she had been the first time she was convicted of a crime?

He knew better than most how many ex-cons fell back into theft. He was often the one who took them in the second time around and listened to their sorry excuses.

"I gave you the biggest piece of cake," Barbara said as he sat down at his place at the table.

"Thank you." Wade smiled. It was the cake of his childhood fantasies, and he was going to have to force himself to eat it. All he wanted to do was take Jasmine home and then park his car at the end of the lane to her father's place. Why did she have to be tied up with Lonnie? Why couldn't she be a nice, ordinary woman like Barbara here? Carl never had to worry about arresting *her*.

Wade felt the smoothness of the cake on his tongue and the sweet tang of the raspberry filling. He smiled up at Barbara and thanked her again for the cake. The two kids at the table were smacking their lips and demanding more, just as Wade would be doing if he wasn't so troubled.

Then he looked down the table and saw his dear friend Edith. She wouldn't be happy about him keeping an eye on anyone. It was clear the older woman was very fond of Jasmine. That, of course, was the problem with being a lawman and trying to have friends. He liked things black and white with no shades of gray. He didn't want to have feelings for the suspect.

By doing his job, he was going to upset Jasmine and everyone else in Dry Creek. For the first time since he'd driven into town, he missed the barren feel of his apartment in Idaho Falls. He knew who he was there.

It didn't take long for Wade to leave the Walls' house, with Jasmine walking in front of him. The night was cold. Jasmine wrapped her arms around her body to keep warm and hurried to his car. He was still nursing that leg of his, so he went more slowly than she did. He made it in good time, though, and as he opened the car door for her, she nodded her thanks and slid into the passenger seat.

The first thing Wade did after he got into the car was to move the dial up on the heater. Snowflakes were just starting to fall, but they were scattered enough that he could clear them away with his windshield wipers.

He silently turned his car around and started down the sheriff's lane. The car lights shone on the falling snow, making the flakes look like pinpricks in the darkness.

"You don't think Lonnie would do something to my father, do you?" Jasmine asked. She looked up at him with eyes full of worry. "Lonnie's not very stable. I wouldn't want anyone around here to be hurt by him."

Wade shrugged. "With all you'd inherit if Elmer were out of the picture—"

Jasmine gasped. "I don't care about the money."

"Lonnie might."

That turned her quiet. He didn't want her to worry, though.

"He won't even have the chance to get close to anyone," Wade assured her. "We'll have the feds all over the place by tomorrow. Lonnie has a better chance of breaking in to Fort Knox than he has of sneaking into Dry Creek."

Wade hoped he wasn't lying. He had no idea what the feds would do. And they might have some completely different theories as to why Lonnie had broken out of prison. It might have nothing at all to do with Jasmine or anyone in Dry Creek.

"You'll be safe," Wade said as he opened his door.

He walked around to the passenger door and opened it. Wade stood by the open car door and watched as Jasmine pulled her coat closer to her body. She wasn't making any move to walk toward the house and he wasn't making any move to let her. Finally Wade reached out and touched her cheek. It was soft and a little damp. She must have been crying when she'd been huddled against the door on the drive out here.

"It'll be okay," he whispered to her as he brought his hand down.

"I'm fine," she said.

He nodded with a slight smile. "I know."

Wade had never kissed a suspect, but he would have done it now if he hadn't thought it would make Jasmine cry even more. She was barely hanging on, and he needed to leave her with her dignity.

"I'll be parked at the end of Elmer's lane if you need me," Wade said as he stepped back from the door. Snow was falling in earnest now, but in his trunk he had a heavy sleeping bag that he used on stakeouts like this. "I'll come to the door in the morning, before I go over to my grandfather's."

"You can't sleep outside all night. It's freezing out here. I'll leave the kitchen door unlocked in case you need to come inside."

"Don't leave anything unlocked. I'll duck into the barn if I need to."

Jasmine nodded.

Wade watched her walk to the kitchen door and go inside the house. Only then did he head back to the driver's door. He wondered if he'd get any sleep tonight.

He was losing his edge. The next thing he knew, he was going to be offering pillows to everyone he arrested and wishing them sweet dreams. When had he turned into a soft touch?

He waited for the light to go out in the kitchen before he started his drive down the lane. He already felt lonely.

* * * * *

Will Jasmine give Wade reason to call
Dry Creek home again?
Find out in
SILENT NIGHT IN DRY CREEK
by Janet Tronstad.
Available in October 2009 from Love Inspired®

For private investigator
Wade Sutton, Dry Creek
holds too many memories—
and none of them fond.
Yet he can't say no when
the sheriff asks him to
watch over a woman
who might be in danger.
Getting to know lovely
Jasmine Hunter just might
give Wade a good reason
to call Dry Creek home
once more….

Look for

Silent Night in Dry Creek

by

Janet Tronstad

Available October
wherever books are sold.

Steeple
Hill®

LI87553

Love Inspired®

HEARTWARMING INSPIRATIONAL ROMANCE

Get more of the heartwarming
inspirational romance stories that
you love and cherish, beginning
in July with SIX NEW titles,
available every month from
the Love Inspired® line.

Also look for our other
Love Inspired® genres, including:

Love Inspired® Suspense:
Enjoy four contemporary tales of intrigue
and romance every month.

Love Inspired® Historical:
Travel to a different time with two powerful
and engaging stories of romance, adventure
and faith every month.

Available every month wherever books are sold,
including most bookstores, supermarkets,
drugstores and discount stores.

www.SteepleHill.com

Steeple
Hill®

LIINCREASE2

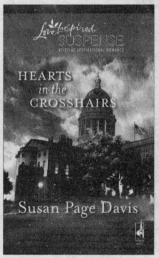

REQUEST YOUR FREE BOOKS!

2 FREE INSPIRATIONAL NOVELS
PLUS 2
FREE
MYSTERY GIFTS

Love Inspired®

YES! Please send me 2 FREE Love Inspired® novels and my 2 FREE mystery gifts (gifts are worth about $10). After receiving them, if I don't wish to receive any more books, I can return the shipping statement marked "cancel". If I don't cancel, I will receive 4 brand-new novels every month and be billed just $4.24 per book in the U.S. or $4.74 per book in Canada. That's a savings of over 20% off the cover price. It's quite a bargain! Shipping and handling is just 50¢ per book.* I understand that accepting the 2 free books and gifts places me under no obligation to buy anything. I can always return a shipment and cancel at any time. Even if I never buy another book, the two free books and gifts are mine to keep forever.

113 IDN EYK2 313 IDN EYLE

Name	(PLEASE PRINT)

Address	Apt. #

City	State/Prov.	Zip/Postal Code

Signature (if under 18, a parent or guardian must sign)

Mail to Steeple Hill Reader Service:

IN U.S.A.: P.O. Box 1867, Buffalo, NY 14240-1867
IN CANADA: P.O. Box 609, Fort Erie, Ontario L2A 5X3

Not valid to current subscribers of Love Inspired books.

**Want to try two free books from another series?
Call 1-800-873-8635 or visit www.morefreebooks.com**

* Terms and prices subject to change without notice. Prices do not include applicable taxes. Sales tax applicable in N.Y. Canadian residents will be charged applicable provincial taxes and GST. Offer not valid in Quebec. This offer is limited to one order per household. All orders subject to approval. Credit or debit balances in a customer's account(s) may be offset by any other outstanding balance owed by or to the customer. Please allow 4 to 6 weeks for delivery. Offer available while quantities last.

Your Privacy: Steeple Hill Books is committed to protecting your privacy. Our Privacy Policy is available online at www.SteepleHill.com or upon request from the Reader Service. From time to time we make our lists of customers available to reputable third parties who may have a product or service of interest to you. If you would prefer we not share your name and address, please check here. ☐

LIREG09

Love Inspired

TITLES AVAILABLE NEXT MONTH

Available September 29, 2009

SILENT NIGHT IN DRY CREEK by Janet Tronstad

Private investigator Wade Sutton plans to hightail it out of Dry Creek long before December 25th. Until he's asked to watch over a woman in danger, a woman whose faith could change him forever.

THE MATCHMAKING PACT by Carolyne Aarsen
After the Storm

Widowed rancher Silas Marstow's young daughter and her best friend are determined to see him and single mother Josie Cane married. *Very* determined!

THE PERFECT GIFT by Lenora Worth

Disoriented after a car crash, Goldie Rios wakes up on Rory Branagan's sofa. All Rory's sons want for Christmas is a new mom, but is this unexpected guest the mother they've been longing for?

BLUEGRASS CHRISTMAS by Allie Pleiter
Kentucky Corners

Desperate to unite a town in crisis through a good old-fashioned Christmas church pageant, Mary Thorpe tries to enlist handsome neighbor Mac McCarthy. But Mac's a holiday humbug. Can Mary bring the spirit of Christmas into his life—and love into his heart?

SOLDIER DADDY by Cheryl Wyatt
Wings of Refuge

Young Sarah Graham surprises everyone by passing U.S. Air Force commander Aaron Petrowski's nanny inspection. Only secrets in her past could destroy the home she's built in his heart.

DREAMING OF HOME by Glynna Kaye

Meg McGuire has unwittingly set her sights on the same job and house as single dad Joe Diaz. Determined to give his young son the best life he can, this military man isn't giving up without a fight. But soon Joe is dreaming of a home with the one woman who could take it all away.

LICNMBPA0909